Live Bait

Cameron Pierce

Severed Press
Hobart Tasmania

Live Bait

Author's Note

I wrote Live Bait while living in Grahamstown, South Africa as the Mellon writer-in-residence at Rhodes University. Grahamstown is a vibrant town full of beautiful decaying cathedrals and lush, green plant life. It's situated on the Eastern Cape, about an hour's drive from the Indian Ocean, and the aquatic life here is unbelievable. The coelacanth, previously believed to be extinct for 65-70 million years, was caught off the coast of South Africa in 1938, and is currently housed in one of the many museums on the Rhodes campus. Since arriving in Grahamstown, I've gone out on two overnight fishing excursions with Morgan, the owner of a local restaurant. On the first outing, we fished the surf of the Indian Ocean through a lightning storm, facing harsh winds and rain. Despite the weather, I caught two guitarfish and a sea-barbel, which is a common species of highly venomous catfish. The eyes of the sea-barbel glow red, making it somewhat frightening even without the knowledge that the venom that coats its spines kills people from time to time. The larger of the two guitarfish went about 40 inches and put up a substantial fight, peeling line and giving my light tackle a workout. There is nothing quite like fishing a strange new ocean in the middle of the night during a lightning storm, and I hope to repeat the experience again. On my second night trip out with Morgan, we pursued sharks. Around three in the morning, with almost no visibility, I did battle with a 200 pound ragged-tooth shark. Thanks to the goodwill of some unknown fishing god, the shark was landed. The sheer muscle of the ragged-tooth is almost supernatural. I'm amazed by their strength, their mouths full of jagged, razor-sharp teeth, and their small, calculating eyes. But sharks are not blood-thirsty killers. You can sense that in the way they strike. There's an initial nose-bump as they test the bait, then they might play with it for a minute or two before committing, at which point they might make the first of several tremendous runs. I'm telling you all this because Live Bait is a book that was written during the darkness of South African nights, under another set of stars that I'm used to, through thunderstorms and monsoon-like rain, but Live Bait is about another place close to my heart: Portland, Oregon, a city whose motto is "Keep Portland Weird."

Live Bait is most certainly a weird book, and throughout, you'll find references to some of my favorite Portland locales, most significantly the stretch of the Eastbank Esplanade that runs underneath Burnside Bridge. It's where I caught my first sturgeon, and also where I tagged my first keeper sturgeon. Fighting monstrous prehistoric fish within a stone's throw of a major metropolitan area, while bicyclists, joggers, transients, and drug dealers pass by is an angling experience totally unique to Portland. In my opinion, there's nothing like it. Live Bait is my tribute to that strange fishing experience and all the other dedicated Esplanade fishermen. A deep, murky river like the Willamette is rife with mystery, and full of life despite the pollution. Fishing the Willamette often proved to be a fruitless labor -- it was a difficult, demanding river -- and where you caught fifty fish one day, you might catch none the next, but those mornings and evenings searching the depths for sturgeon, those were some of the best, most bizarre fishing days of all my life. Like the Willamette and the city of Portland, Live Bait is an oddity, inspired by the television show River Monsters and aquatic creature features like Piranha and post-apocalyptic freak-outs like John Dies at the End (David Wong) and Skullcrack City (Jeremy Robert Johnson), but for unknown reasons I also had Charles Bukowski on my mind while writing this book. In terms of structure, two of Richard Brautigan's novels, A Confederate General from Big Sur and The Abortion, served as my road map through the strange terrain explored here. And then there's the Lovecraftian influence....

The bottom line is, Live Bait might be the weirdest aquatic horror story ever written, one that's equal parts pulp angling action, debauched bender, and absurdist apocalyptic fantasy. The writing of it has been an equally odd process, what with the birds screaming at four every morning and the hyena cackling a few nights back. All this is to say thanks for taking the ride with me. Live Bait has been one hell of a trip. I hope you enjoy it. Your support means the world.

Cameron Pierce
Grahamstown, South Africa
24 February 2015

The Gospel of Gordon West

My name is Gordon West. By the time you read this, I'll be dead. I'm writing all this down should anyone care to know how the world ended, or at least my personal account of the end. I don't have much time left. They'll come for me soon. At least they've placed me in a cell alone, with enough light and the pencil and paper I requested. There's a guard outside my cell, but he won't bother me so long as I keep quiet and don't attempt to kill myself. In the interest of completion, I will record everything I can before morning. Then it's my time to go. This is my final night on earth. What am I doing with it? I'm telling you that friendship is a killer. If you're not careful, it might just help bring about the end of the world. Welcome to my gospel. Buckle up. We don't have much time.

Live Bait

Friendship at the End of the World

Live Bait

The Loneliness of the Midsummer Sturgeon Hunter

The alarm clock went off at a quarter to four. My head pounded with the malt liquor I hadn't yet metabolized. Bones groaned from a week of overtime on the new high-rise construction site downtown. I lacked the strength to rise, but I thought of prehistoric fish and a little light glowed hot inside me. My first weekend off in two weeks. Today I was going fishing.

I descended the ladder of the creaking loft bed, downed an energy drink in the dark. I gathered up my fishing gear and the bait sack from the fridge, then stepped out of the studio apartment into the brisk pre-dawn air. Except for some bums sleeping in doorways, downtown Portland was dark and empty. I lit a cigarette, hoping it would burn away the impending hangover.

I could've driven to the river, but I loved walking through the city in the desolate hours, pacing the cold, dark tail-end of a summer night.

The sturgeon gear was heavy and awkward to carry. A twelve-foot rod with a reel twice the size of my fist, a large nylon net with an extendable metal handle, several pounds of squid and herring in the bait bag, and a duffel containing a buck knife, pliers, headlamp, and terminal tackle.

On the walk over Morrison Bridge, several boats sped along the river beneath, vanishing either upriver to Oregon City or downriver to Multnomah

Channel, but none of the boats anchored up anywhere near the Esplanade in Portland Harbor, where I planned to fish. I sent off a silent prayer to the sturgeon gods and quickened my pace.

Minutes before five, I finally arrived at my favorite fishing hole. From the other end of the floating walkway, another lone sturgeon fisherman was also arriving.

I set down my gear well south of the other fisherman, alone, at the spot where the river depth dropped from thirty feet to eighty-plus. I rigged up with a whole squid, my go-to bait on most occasions. The tide was slack and hardly moving. Not ideal sturgeon conditions, but tides always changed and I had all day.

Following my first cast, I checked the time on my phone. 5:03. Too nervous and cold to sit down, I lit a cigarette and paced, keeping a watchful eye on my pole for the familiar *tap-tap* of a sturgeon testing the bait with its vacuum-like mouth. Across the river, the neon *Welcome to Portland* sign flashed. Even when the fishing was slow, the Esplanade was one of my favorite places to be in the early hours. Some nights I went straight there from the bars just to watch the whole town come alive, before drunkenly stumbling home to bed.

Over the next hour and a half, the bite was dead. Something bit a chunk out of a herring, but the teeth marks and the suddenness of the short strike suggested a species other than sturgeon, most likely a bullhead.

The sun was coming up now and I began succumbing to the hangover, which thudded between my ears, making total agony of consciousness. I was resigning to a slow fishing day, even weighing the benefits of turning in early, beating back the hangover with a cold beer, when suddenly the ice was broken.

The guy fishing to the right of me, about thirty yards away, hooked into a sturgeon. The guy's rod – a stout, yellow antique – buckled over. I looked on with the heart-thudding anticipation reserved for those who pursue big game. Every fish could be a giant.

This fish turned out to be a shaker, maybe two feet long and well short of legal size. By the time the man had returned the fish to the river, I turned my focus back to my own rod. I was feeling increasingly desperate, more so now that I was running low on cigarettes.

I lit one of my last cigarettes off the one before. That's when my rod buckled. I waited for a second full takedown before setting the hook and feeling the affirmation of a fish on the other end. The sturgeon fought hard, diving deep several times.

Cigarette pinched between my lips, smoke drifted up and made my eyes water, but I squinted against the sting and focused entirely on the fish, trying to anticipate its next movements. The sturgeon tore off on a run. I gained back line again before the fish made another run. We went back and forth like that until finally the great fish broke the surface, leaping fully out of the water, displaying its snow-white belly and sharp diamond scutes for all the world to see.

I loosened the drag in case the sturgeon made a

last ditch effort at freedom. With the pole in my left hand, I took the large net in my right, leaned over the railing, and scooped up the defeated fish. But already I could tell it was not a keeper. I tossed it back in the river and baited up again, confidence restored.

Little time passed before my rod bowed again. I reeled up another shaker and tossed it back.

The fishing slowed. Another half hour passed. I snubbed out my last cigarette and set about retying a new rig. That was when the fisherman down the way started yelling. At first it was hard for me to make out what he was saying, but the way his rod was bent into a horseshoe clarified everything. He was shouting, "Net! Net! Net!"

I grabbed my net and hurried over. I kept my distance to give the man room to fight the fish, net poised so that when the fish rose, I'd be in position. But the water there was eighty feet deep, and the fish wasn't giving up ground easily. The man rode the fish hard. His drag looked too tight and I worried he was going to break off. Longing for another cigarette, blood pounding in my ears, I held my breath. The fight was almost over.

Bubbles boiled on the surface, followed by a fat keeper sturgeon, likely a fifty incher.

I lowered my net over the railing and down into the water to scoop up the trophy fish, but as soon as the nylon netting brushed against the sturgeon's gray, diamond-studded back, it took off again and bolted straight down into deep water.

"Shit, man, I'm sorry," I said.

The man looked pissed, but he didn't express it.

"No worries. I'll get her back up," he said, while the fish peeled off line, heading straight for the bottom and out toward the shipping channel. The long run tired the great fish though, and soon the man fought it back to the floating dock. It thrashed its tail in futility as it rose to the surface. I was set on not bungling the net job this time.

The fish rolled belly-up, exhausted. Except for the snow-white belly, the fish was as gray as a Portland day. It looked like a defeated god. The gills worked overtime. The tubular mouth protruded, stuffed with a whole herring. I observed all this in mere moments, and in one swift motion, I plunged the big net into the water and raised it up from beneath the fish. I lifted the net, muscles straining and heart thudding faster as I felt the tremendous weight of the fish.

I heaved the sturgeon upward, but just before the net swung over the high railing, a massive boil appeared on the surface of the water underneath the sturgeon. With the swiftness of a black mamba striking prey, the head of a gargantuan beast rose up and swallowed the sturgeon whole. The monster's teeth tore through the net like it was made of cobwebs. The hooked jaws of the terrible fish were scarred and mottled green and brown, filled with teeth larger than a man's fingers. It engulfed the four-foot-long sturgeon as if it were a baitfish.

The man screamed obscenities as the monster vanished in the mud-colored river with his catch, and I was left holding a mangled, empty net.

"What the fuck was that?" the man shouted. "What the fuck?"

Judging by its jaws, I would've guessed that it was a muskie, but muskie didn't live in the Willamette, and muskie didn't grow to be twenty feet long. Based on the size of its head, and the ease with which the thing gulped down a good-sized sturgeon, the monster was *at least* twenty feet long.

The whole scenario had pretty much knocked the hangover right out of me. I could barely contain my excitement, or the trembling of my hands. Sturgeon over ten feet still lurked in the river, and in days now gone there had been sturgeon over twenty feet long. However, the days of twenty-foot-long sturgeon had ended more than a century ago, when rich San Franciscans developed a taste for caviar. Besides, sturgeons were more scavengers and bottom feeders than upper food chain predators.

The man who'd nearly landed the sturgeon lit up a cigarette. "I swear, this river is cursed," he said. "My name's Bob, by the way."

"Mind if I bum a cigarette?"

The man fumbled at the breast pocket of his flannel shirt for his cigarettes, slid one out and handed it to me.

I stuck the cigarette between my lips and reached for my lighter, but Bob held his own lighter up to the cigarette.

I hated when people lit cigarettes for me. The flame always felt hotter when I wasn't in control. I didn't protest. I'd gotten a cigarette, after all.

After a deep, lung-choking drag, I said, "I'm Gordon West."

Bob nodded in acknowledgment of this, and we smoked in silence, processing what had occurred.

When my cigarette burned down to a stub, I crushed it beneath my boot and nodded, having settled on a plan in my mind. "We have to catch it," I said.

"If you want to go after that thing with anything less than the Marines, then I'd say you're crazy."

"So what do you say?"

"I'd say it's nice to meet you, but you're crazy."

"You in, or you out?"

Bob stood there, clearly replaying the scene in his mind, the monster rising up from the river and chowing down on the netted sturgeon. "Man, we can't go after that thing. This ain't fucking *Moby-Dick*," he said.

It was the fastest and most ferocious animal attack I had ever seen in my life, and I'd seen plenty of great whites in action during the time I spent as a deckhand on a yellowfin charter off the coast of South Africa.

"Guess you're right," I said, the initial excitement of the encounter now fading as reality set in. Odds of ever seeing the river monster again were slim to nothing. I figured I'd gotten my one good glimpse at something truly unknown.

"Tell you what, though," Bob said, "I could really go for a beer after that."

I held up my ruined net. "Well, since I lost your fish, I guess that means first round's on me."

Green Dragon

We loaded our fishing gear into the back of Bob's tan Land Rover, decked out with roll bars and off-road tires as if ready for the safari.

In the Land Rover, I noticed the name MELINDA carved into the dashboard, and I asked about it.

Bob sighed heavily. "Melinda. Let me tell you about Melinda. That's what her previous owner named her, and the name sort of stuck. I used to do trail work outside Juno and Skagway, up in Alaska. I did it every summer for six years. My last year, I realized I didn't have anything to return to at the end of trail season, so I decided to get my own place, live in Alaska year-round. Two months after the rest of the trail crew left, my first two months of Alaskan winter, I wanted to kill myself. I grew up in Brooklyn. Cold weather never bothered me. But Alaskan winters are different. The darkness of the Alaskan winter is smothering. The wetness turns you mushy, softens your bones. It doesn't help that everyone else is going bug-fuck crazy around you too. After two months in hell, I bought Melinda off a bar owner who'd drunk his own bar dry. I was going mad. I wasn't making sound decisions. I drove Melinda from Skagway down through British Columbia. I never stopped except for gas and coffee until I reached Portland. I'd never been to Portland before, but I haven't ever left since then either. And this baby got me here."

"That's a hell of a story for a Land Rover," I said.

"She's never broken down on me. Never caused me any problems. I figure I owe it to her to tell the full story."

"You're not married, are you, Bob?"

Bob laughed a little. "No, I'm not. It never happened for me."

"Yeah, that whole boat passed me by as well."

"Far as I'm concerned, I'm happily married to Melinda."

"Yeah, but she's an automobile."

"Hey, it's the twenty-first century. Who's judging?"

"So where you wanna grab a beer?"

"I don't know. What about Sassy's?" Bob said.

"Won't your wife get mad about you going to a strip club?"

"That's the best thing about being married to a Land Rover. She never gets jealous."

We laughed together. I felt like I was beginning to make a friend.

"I'm not really much into strip clubs," I said. "You ever hit up Green Dragon?"

"No, where's that?"

"It's a beer hall off Belmont, not far from here. Looks like a greenhouse or a miniature airplane hangar."

"I'm game for that," Bob said.

"Then let's roll!"

Bob started up Melinda, her engine purring like a jungle cat in heat, and we pulled onto Burnside Bridge. A song by Hank Williams Sr. came on the radio. The song, about a wooden Indian who falls in love, was a favorite of mine. I started to sing along, and then Bob turned the radio up real loud and joined in, and we belted out the name of that heartbroken wooden Indian.

*

Green Dragon was packed when we arrived, typical of most Portland beer houses at noon on a Saturday, but we found a bench on the smoking patio out back. I went up to the bar and ordered a round of Gigantic IPAs. I wasn't sure if Bob liked hoppy beer, but Gigantic was great and I figured the name suited the occasion.

I sat down at the bench across from Bob, who was giving dirty looks to the hipsters at the tables around us. "This is why I stick to real bars," Bob said, gesturing to the crowds of bearded young men in flannel and tattooed young women with asymmetric haircuts.

"Shut up and drink your beer," I said, taking a pull off the foamy head of my IPA.

Bob picked up his pint glass, sipped off the top, and made a bitter beer face.

"Don't tell me you only drink shit domestics," I said.

"No." Bob shook his head, tried the IPA again, still clearly dissatisfied. "King Cobra's more my speed."

"Shit, man. I'm sorry," I said. "Let me get you another beer."

Bob gestured as if to say it was no trouble, but I insisted. Finally, Bob relented and allowed me to go in and get him another beer. They didn't have any cheap domestics, so I got him the lightest lager they had on tap.

Back at the table again, Bob approving of his beer, he said, "So what's your story?"

I unconsciously reached for a cigarette before remembering I was out. Luckily Bob noticed the gesture and provided one. He even let me light my own this time. I took a deep drag and contemplated which version of myself I wanted to sell. Bob seemed like a good person, someone who could become a great friend, so I settled on the truest version of myself I could manage to tell without feeling like a piece of shit. "I grew up in a backwoods nowhere town north of Seattle. I loved to fish, but I hated the cold, the constant rain. At a too-young age, I discovered that I liked getting fucked up. I mean really loaded. On anything. Any time. But drugs are an expensive hobby, especially for a high school kid whose family is on welfare. I decided to start selling. I figured if I could move just enough weed that I basically smoked for free, it was an even trade. Turns out I'm good at hustling. I could get high every day and still turn a profit. I bought my first car off pot earnings when I was seventeen. Within a year of high school graduation, I'd scored connections in Seattle so I could start moving cocaine, MDMA, LSD, mushrooms, and occasionally shit like DMT and ketamine.

"Fast forward a bit and here I was, this nineteen-year-old drug dealer, living large, basically fishing around the clock because I was so fucking high all the time and being a dealer allowed me the freedom to work from anywhere. I mean, most of the people I sold to would meet me on the Skykomish or whatever other river I was fishing that day. It was perfect. The Department of Fish and Wildlife is understaffed and overworked as it is, so the last thing they're thinking of doing is busting a drug deal out on the water. No, they're too busy worrying about poachers and catching people out there without licenses. The bottom tray in my tackle box was full of drugs. As I said, perfect.

"I had this cocktail of drugs I called Salmon Slayer. A bowl of high-grade weed, two lines of coke, and a low dose of mushrooms. I felt like it turned me into a fish, or part fish. It gave me this tremendous focus, so that standing on the river and fishing for twelve hours straight felt like minutes. Better than that, I really believed it attuned me to the fish way of thinking. I believed I was part fish. Maybe I did become part fish, because I swear to God, high out of my mind like that, I seemed to always know what the fish were after. Like I could read their fish minds. But then one day pursuing steelhead in December, I double-dosed on Salmon Slayer and ended up stripping naked, wading out into the river, and masturbating violently. I guess I believed I'd turned into a steelhead and was spawning. Luckily I hadn't caught any fish that day because I might've tried to fuck it.

"Anyway, that got me arrested for public indecency and public intoxication. Some miracle prevented the cops from inspecting my tackle bag, or I would've been seriously fucked. Instead, they put me under psychiatric evaluation for three weeks because they believed I'd been trying to kill myself.

And who knows. Maybe I was. Wading into the river in December, completely fried like that, I should've died.

"Somehow in my fucked-up state, I'd still retained a shred of intelligence. When the cops grilled me about what I was on, I guess I'd told them I was drunk and stoned. Marijuana was already almost legal in Washington by this time, so there wasn't much incentive to pin charges on someone for being stoned.

"Looking back, I think the only thing that prevented them from searching my shit is one of the cops who arrested me. He was a fisherman himself and had seen me on the rivers a lot. Even in the fried state I was in, I'd recognized him when he stepped out of the squad car and came down to the river. One day, I'd given my only salmon to him and his son. I had no idea he was a cop at the time. I was just high on MDMA and experienced a deep wave of empathy for this guy who was trying and failing to get his son hooked on fishing. Man, I was so messed up during this time. I'm rambling now."

"No, go on," Bob said. He was genuinely listening. He'd hardly touched his lager.

I slammed back my IPA, reached for the one Bob had refused to drink. "I'd always hated my hometown. The constant damp of it. The dark winter days. Unfortunately, drug dealers don't have much of a fallback plan. I spent three weeks in the psych ward. That meant three weeks without pay. My clientele was pissed. My suppliers were pissed. Friends? I learned I had none. Family? My arrest spread to the local news, then went viral on the internet. Even my parents disowned me over the embarrassment it caused. When I got out, I bailed on my apartment and broke the lease on my F-150. I used a chunk of what remaining funds I had to buy a ticket to Johannesburg. I had an old aunt in South Africa who could vouch for me, which was fortunately enough to get me a visa. The American dollar was strong against the rand, so my dwindling cash would go further down there. Better yet, I couldn't dream of a place more unlike my hometown than South Africa.

"Joburg ate me alive in under two weeks, so I migrated toward the coast and found work on a yellowtail charter boat. That was decent for a while, but rich tourists are the biggest pains in the ass. I couldn't handle them. Eventually I migrated back to the states, where ugliness is the standard and therefore invisible."

"So why Portland?" Bob said.

I shrugged. "I don't know. Guess I always liked the Trail Blazers."

There was silence between us. Then I sort of laughed and said, "So I'm the drug-dealing expat and you're the Alaskan runaway who loves his car too much."

Bob smiled. "I guess maybe we're the perfect team to track down this river monster."

Talking about my past and having a beer with a new friend had resulted in me almost entirely forgetting about the encounter on the river. The monster seemed so distant. I remembered we had come here with a purpose.

"First thing's first," I said. "More beer."

Bob nodded. "Let's do it."

"Second thing. If this monster is some sort of a giant muskie, which it appeared to be, then we need to gather all the facts we can about muskie."

"Sounds good, Sherlock."

"I'm gonna join the dark side and have a stout," I said. "You want another lager?"

"You know what?" Bob said. "I've never had a stout. I think I'll join you on the dark side."

Six hours and a dozen beers later, we were both shit-face drunk but no closer to figuring out how to track down the river monster.

"You know," Bob said, his eyes half-closed, his head bobbing with drunkenness, "when I look back on the days behind me, I don't think so much about the girls I dated or the places I visited. Except maybe Alaska. But fuck Alaska." He laughed drunkenly and raised his pint glass to his lips, spilling stout down his chin. "I think more about the docks I fished year after year. A good fishing dock is hard to find."

"Damn right it is," I said.

"Time and circum...circumcision? No, that's not right. Time and...fuck, what's the word I'm looking for?"

"I think you mean circumstance."

"That's it. A good fishing dock is a thing of time and circumstance. That's what makes all docks beautiful."

"But some are more beautiful than others," I said, sliding a cigarette from Bob's pack, which sat on the table between us.

"So what's the most beautiful dock you ever

fished?" Bob asked.

I pondered the question before responding. "I'd have to say the gazebo behind the library on Lake Stevens. My brother and I used to fish for yellow perch there every day in the summer. God, I miss those days."

Bob was too drunk to acknowledge my answer and carried on as though he had not asked the question. "The boat docks at Buena Vista, man. They were like an old woman's hand. Gnarled. Arthritic. Docks were so fucking warped you could hardly stand on them, but if you went out to the furthest dock and stood carefully, and cast straight out, and it happened to be a warm summer night when the mosquitoes weren't too thick, you could catch fat channel catfish. Blue catfish too. I caught the biggest blue cat of my life from that far, gnarled dock. On mornings in November and December, brown trout congregated off the docks and my father and I caught them with Rooster Tails. It'd be just us out there. The fog used to fill the valley so thick in the fall and winter that the drive to the lake was just like driving through bottle glass worn smooth and murky by the sea."

I had used my last match and needed to borrow Bob's lighter, which was in the pocket of Bob's jeans, but Bob was on a drunken roll now, speaking more eloquently than he might have on the same subject sober, the paradox of the heavy drinker. Goddamn, I wanted a cigarette. And yet Bob kept on talking.

"The spring is when the action really picked up at the docks. Crappie jigs slayed the slabs and bluegill. Carp spawned in the shallows, moseying around the docks like finned bars of gold, but we left the carp alone to spawn. What more did anyone need but a million panfish on a dewy spring morning? Maybe a cold Pepsi, but we packed an ice chest. Then in the summer the catfishing picked up again. That old woman's hand of a boat dock kept track of the seasons for us. She pointed us toward the future. Eventually she got so old, they tore off her hand, our sacred fishing docks."

"Bob."

"The fish stopped biting there after that, and a drought came and never went away so the lake dried up. When I die, I expect to walk hand-in-hand with the ghost of the Buena Vista docks. Or, if not..."

"Bob!"

"What?"

"Lemme see your lighter."

"Oh, shit. Sorry man. You should've said something."

Bob handed his lighter over to me. I lit up the cigarette I'd been rolling between my fingers and took a deep drag.

"So what about our river monster?" I asked.

"Our gear's still in Melinda. It'll be dark soon."

"I wasn't saying we go back down there now."

"Why not?"

"Why? That thing would chew through braided line like it was linguine. Even if it didn't, it'd spool us."

"We don't need to catch it...just draw it in."

"I'm not following," I said.

"Think of the sea lions at Willamette Falls."

"What about them?"

"They've learned that when someone grabs a net or jumps for a fishing rod, it means there's a salmon feast just waiting there for them, ready to be snatched off the line."

"Yeah, those furbags cost me a lot of springers last year."

"What if our monster is the same? Maybe it got lost, came up from the Pacific into the mouth of the Columbia, then just kept on swimming all the way to Portland, into the Willamette, lurking among the deepest holes..."

"Like the hole under Burnside Bridge."

"And we can keep it there by holding food captive."

I wasn't convinced. "The size of that thing, if it wanted to munch on some sturgeon, it would have no trouble chasing them down."

"Yeah, but think about it. There aren't a hell of a lot of sturgeon in the Willy this time of year. The water's too warm. Most of the oversize fish are out at sea. That's gonna leave slim pickings for our big mama. Plus, the modus operandi of all fish is energy conservation. If it happens to still be hanging around Burnside, maybe we can convince it to hang around by offering easy meals."

The light finally clicked on for me. "Like how the sea lions learned that salmon fishermen would do the hard work for them."

"Exactly. We put sturgeon on the line, fight them slowly, and maybe, just maybe, the river monster takes a liking to the sluggish food source."

"That sounds okay in theory, but I don't know," I

said. "It's kind of fucked up. I mean, the sturgeon population isn't exactly booming. How many fish would we be offering up as snacks?"

"Imagine how many it'll eat if we don't stop it. That thing could be the end of sturgeon as we know them." Bob looked very serious as he said this, his eyes bugged out, his lips quivering with drunken rage. He looked ridiculous.

"So this is a conservation effort?" I asked, but Bob's head suddenly drooped. His forehead hit the lip of his beer glass, spilling the remains of his stout. Asleep in a puddle of beer, he began to snore.

I went inside and settled our tab. I'd paid for all our beers, but that was fine. I was happy to have made another craft beer convert. Better than that, I'd made a friend. I called a taxi.

I gathered up Bob from the smoking patio and helped him outside. We sat on the curb and waited for the cab.

"Melinda..." Bob slurred.

"Melinda will be fine parked here tonight, man. We're in no state to drive."

"I miss her so much..."

I got the impression that Melinda used to be someone else in Bob's life besides his Land Rover. I filed the thought away as something to inquire about later, perhaps when I knew Bob a bit better. It's sad to think now that time would never come.

I smoked the rest of Bob's cigarettes while waiting for the cab, which was extremely late, as Portland cabs usually were.

When it finally arrived, I pushed Bob into the back seat and rolled in after him. I gave the driver my address and we sped through the desolate industrial district before heading over Burnside Bridge, right over the spot where we'd encountered the river monster that morning. The city lights glimmered on the surface of the river, but all was calm and quiet, as if the river and all its denizens were dreaming.

Back at my apartment, I made a bed for Bob on the couch. Bob mumbled a thank you and a request for a glass of water. I filled a glass and Bob guzzled it sloppily, spilling half on himself and the couch.

I turned on the computer and checked my online dating profile, hoping for a new message from that rock climbing chick I'd been talking to. We'd exchanged messages back and forth all week, but after I asked her out for a cup of coffee, she'd gone silent. Seeing no response from her and no other new messages, I climbed up into the loft bed and fell asleep.

Bloody Sunday

I stirred in bed around one in the afternoon. It was Sunday. I looked down over the railing of the loft bed.

Bob had rolled off the couch at some point during the night and was asleep on the floor.

I climbed the ladder out of the loft bed and went into the kitchen, which was more of a closet with a stove, to cook breakfast, or lunch, or whatever you call it when you wake up and the day is half done. I scrambled eggs and fried up some bacon. I didn't own a toaster -- there wasn't room for it -- so I baked four slices of bread in the oven to crispness. I boiled water for coffee and ground the beans I'd picked up from a local roaster. I knew it was a funny thing about myself. When it came to beer, I'd drink everything from malt liquor to the finest, most esoteric craft ales, and I could find merit in it all. The merit was that it got me drunk. Coffee was another story. I couldn't handle the cheap shit. No Folgers. No Yuban. No instant either. I needed good, whole coffee beans, ground fresh. It was a habit I picked up while living in South Africa. I still missed the cafes there.

The kettle whistled and I poured it over the beans into the French press. While the coffee steeped, I slid eggs and bacon onto two plates. I plucked the toast from the oven.

"Breakfast's up," I said.

"What time is it?" Bob groaned, his head half-covered by a blanket.

"Almost two in the afternoon. Now up and at 'em."

"Oh, fuck. I was supposed to be at work."

"Where do you work?"

Bob sat up, rubbed his eyes like he was trying to juice his brain. His hangover must've been savage. "Wait, what day is it?" he asked.

"Sunday."

"Nevermind. I don't work Sundays."

I depressed the lever on the French press and poured two mugs of coffee. "Drink some of this. It'll help with your head."

Bob accepted the mug gratefully and took a sip. "Mmm...that's good shit," he said. His eyes almost opened all the way. Then alertness hit and he looked around, alarmed. "Wait, how'd we get here? I didn't drive, did I?"

I shook my head. "No, I called us a cab. Melinda's safe, up on Belmont where we parked."

Relief washed over Bob. "Good. I can't handle another DUI."

"Nobody can, brother. That's why I don't drive," I said. I brought the two plates piled high with eggs, bacon, and toast over to the small metal folding table near the defunct fireplace. "Come on, let's eat. We got a busy day ahead of us."

Bob pulled himself off the floor, groaning, joints popping. He sat down beside me at the small table. "I gotta ask you something, Gordon."

"Go for it."

"Why's your apartment look like a twenty-year-old girl from Brooklyn decorated it?"

I looked around. The loft bed. The canary yellow

sofa I'd dragged in off a street corner. The black and white tiled floor. The pale blue walls. The built-in bookshelves (although ninety-five percent of the books I owned were about fishing). The French press. And draped over the street-front window, the yellow curtains. The curtains matched the couch, but that was entirely coincidental. I'd seriously dragged that couch in off the street. It looked nice, but that didn't mean bums hadn't fucked on it. They had. I'd chased them away so I could haul the couch home for myself. They ran down the street, pants around their ankles, and I took home the couch and wiped off the spots of bum cum with a wet rag. That shit was so not designer, even though it looked it.

"Bob..." I began. "I don't have an answer for you. My apartment looks the way it does because that's how it looks."

"Did you have like, a girlfriend who decorated it for you? I'm just wondering."

"Well stop wondering and eat your goddamn breakfast."

Underwater Steakhouse

After breakfast, we caught a bus back to Southeast Portland to retrieve Melinda. Memories hazy, we circled several blocks before locating her. The smell hit us as soon as we climbed inside. It'd been a hot evening and the morning temperature already hovered around eighty-five. We had forgotten to remove our bait from Melinda, and now she smelled like the dumpster outside a fish processing facility. We hopped out of the Land Rover and stood around it, wondering how we could endure the smell.

"Sorry, girl," Bob said, as if Melinda could smell the spoiled bait too.

We tossed the bait in a trashcan and rolled down all the windows before driving to Ollie Damon's to restock. Even with the windows down, the odor of rotted squid and herring was almost unbearable.

"It's funny that we've been going to the same tackle shop for years and never ran into each other," Bob said.

"I fish mostly with squid, and I buy that at the Asian market," I said. I hesitated for a moment, then continued, "And to be honest, I buy most of my terminal tackle online. It's cheaper and the selection is better."

"Can't blame you," Bob said.

We pulled up outside Ollie Damon's, which was only a few blocks from Green Dragon. Driving there was sort of absurd, but we were hungover so we'd done it anyway. Ollie Damon's was closed though.

"Shit, it's Sunday," Bob said. "I forgot again."

"Well, what do you want to do?"

"It's your call."

"We can drive out to Fisherman's Marine, or Cabela's in Tualatin. Or we can grab a spicy Bloody Mary at My Father's Place."

"As nice as a Bloody Mary sounds, I think we need to hit the river."

"Yeah, you're probably right," I said.

"But a *spicy* Bloody Mary..."

*

We stumbled out of the dark bar into the fading light. One spicy Bloody Mary apiece had turned into three, and then we lost track of time. The heat rose from the asphalt in waves. The coming evening did nothing to dissipate it. The wind that always blew off the river at this hour would keep the Esplanade cool. If only we could remember where we parked again.

"I'm too loaded to drive," Bob said.

"Fuck it, let's just walk to the river. It's only a couple blocks."

"What bait've we got?"

"We'll stop at the store. Pick up some steaks."

"Steaks?"

"Yeah. You got a problem with steaks?"

"I thought we were supposed to lure the river monster in with sturgeon on the line. We can't actually catch the damned thing."

"We need a better plan," I said. "I propose steaks."

"I don't understand, but if you want to fish with steaks, we can fish with steaks."

"Goddamn right we can."

After another half hour searching, we found Melinda parked around the corner. We unloaded our cumbersome sturgeon gear and marched up Grand Avenue to the neighborhood grocery mart, where we purchased six sirloin steaks, a twelve pack of Pabst Blue Ribbon, and a bag of Funyuns. Outside the grocery mart, we realized we hadn't eaten since breakfast, so we popped into the food cart pod in the parking lot down the street and ordered tacos from a taco truck. We sat and ate the tacos as the sun went down. By the time we stumbled the handful of blocks to the river, it was already dark. The Esplanade was well-lit, and across the river, the Portland stag sign flickered on.

The river was turgid, almost at a standstill, so we tied on new rigs with four ounce pyramid weights and the largest octopus hooks we owned. Threading hooks through sirloin wasn't easy, but we managed two hooks per steak. When we each had a steak securely at the end of our lines, we took turns casting out into the depths. I cast first. The steak arced high over the water, casting a dark reflection on the surface of the river, and went under with a tremendous splash. I fed line out, allowing the steak to sink the eighty-plus feet to the bottom.

Bob let a bicyclist pass by, then reared back to cast. Instead of flinging his steak out into the water, he set his rod down. "Almost forgot something," he said.

He fiddled around in his fishing bag and pulled

out a bottle of bait scent. "Every fish loves anise," he said.

I nodded approval. I sort of regretted not scenting my own steak with anise, but I'd cast it out there so nicely, I wasn't about to reel it up so quick. Besides, who knew if the river monster even liked anise?

Bob's steak dripped anise juice as he launched it out into the middle of the river. I cracked open a Pabst. Bob set down his rod on the rail beside mine and took a beer of his own from the twelve pack.

We sat there in the silence, drinking cheap beer, munching on Funyuns, unable to see each other's faces in the darkness, watching our rods for movement, like watching an alien planet for any sign of life.

"Think we'll ever see it again?" Bob asked.

"No," I said.

Bob grunted, as if he was too disappointed to respond with words.

"No," I said, "but I think we'll see it *and* catch it."

"What makes you so sure?"

"I think it's our destiny."

"I'm not much of a believer in destiny, man."

"I'm not either. Or I should say, I wasn't. Seeing that thing rise up and swallow your sturgeon like a Goldfish cracker, that's got a lot of my positions on life going haywire. Maybe I've been thinking backwards or too small-minded all this time. Maybe I don't know what I want."

"I think I get what you mean," Bob said.

"You do?"

"Yeah, and I'm with you. Let's catch this sucker."

Half an hour later, the tip of Bob's rod began to twitch. Much too small of a twitch to be the river monster, but at this point, a couple beers in, we were beginning to regret our decision to fish with steaks. Any action, even the slightest passing interest from a sculpin or pikeminnow, was welcome.

The rod twitch intensified until finally Bob decided to reel up. "Probably bullhead or sculpin pecking at the steak," he said.

The steak's weight put a good bend in the rod as he reeled it in. When the steak came over the rail, a massive crayfish came with it. The crayfish clung to the steak with a powerful claw the size of a man's hand. The crayfish was oxblood red and pissed off. It continued gripping the steak with one claw and lashed out at Bob with the other.

"That thing's bigger than a Maine lobster," I said.

Bob was making high-pitched noises like he'd just won the lottery and couldn't believe it.

"Shit man, this is a superfund site," I said. "You think that has something to do with it? I mean, yesterday's monster and now *this*? That's gotta be the biggest crawdad in the world. You just caught a world record, man. I mean, if there *is* a line-caught crayfish record to break. I think it's time we call ODFW."

Bob couldn't compose himself enough to address the two-foot-long crustacean at our feet.

That's when the screams reached us from downriver.

The Crayfish Makes a Getaway

Between Burnside Bridge and Morrison Bridge, there was a large rocky ledge that jutted out into the river. The ledge was flat and perfect for picnics and campfires. It provided coverage for smallmouth bass to ambush young salmonids and other unassuming prey. I used to fish there often before I discovered the deep hole under Burnside. The ledge was a popular swimming spot in the summer as well because a submerged rock shelf, one to four feet below the surface depending on the tide, allowed people to sit or stand in the river without having to wade in deep water or risk stepping on fish hooks or broken glass in the shallows. The screams led Bob and me to the ledge.

We carried our fishing gear, along with the giant crayfish, which Bob had stuffed claws-down into the now-empty Pabst box. The tail of the crayfish hung out, but at least it couldn't snap at us or anything.

By the time we arrived at the ledge, two young women, soaked from a recent dip, were holding a third young woman on the ground. She flailed at them, wailing in desperation, clawing her way toward the water.

"Everything okay here?" I asked.

"Call the police!" the girl who was being restrained said.

I was a little surprised that no one else had stopped to help them, but then again, Portland was a timid city.

"We'll call 911, but we need to know what kind of assistance you need," I said.

"Her boyfriend drowned," one of the women said.

"He didn't drown," the one on the ground said, "he was eaten by a giant fish!"

She resumed her hysterics before I could push her for more information. Judging by the blood on her bikini, she was telling the truth. I knew the river monster had to be responsible.

Bob pulled out his phone and dialed 911, but instead of putting the phone to his ear, he started muttering to himself and thrust the phone into my hand. I started to ask him, "What the fuck?" Before I could get an answer, the emergency operator's voice interrupted the ring tone and asked if I needed police, the fire department, or an ambulance.

"Police and an ambulance," I said, even though I couldn't really see what the police might do about the giant killer fish.

The operator transferred me to EMS but remained on the line to pass our emergency along to a police dispatcher.

"What is the location of your emergency?" the EMS dispatcher asked.

"We're at the Eastbank Esplanade," I said. "Between Morrison and Burnside Bridge."

"Can you repeat that?" the EMS dispatcher asked.

"Did I fucking stutter?"

"Sir, I'm going to need you to repeat your location."

I felt sort of bad, so I told them again where we

were located.

They asked me all sorts of dumbass questions after that. Can I lead them to the victim when they arrive? No, he was eaten by a giant fucking fish. What is my phone number? Look it up. You've got caller ID. It was Bob's phone and I didn't know the number, so I had to ask him. He didn't know it either. They went ahead and asked what the nature of the emergency was. I told them that some dude drowned, even though I didn't believe for a second that's what really happened.

"Is he conscious or breathing?" the EMS dispatcher asked.

"I don't fucking know. Can he breathe underwater?" I asked.

There was a beat of silence on the other end before the dispatcher finally asked, "And what is your name, sir?"

"Gordon," I said.

They promised to send officers and an ambulance, and I hung up.

"They're sending officers and an ambulance," I said, handing the phone back to Bob.

The restrained woman began weeping quietly to herself, as if the futility of saving an eaten man was finally sinking in.

Her friends whispered to her about how sorry they were, and I found the whole thing distasteful. There was no sorry in the world that could bring her boyfriend back. People always wanted to fill the space of their sorrow with babble, with apologies, when silence was the only adequate form of sorry. When someone said, "I'm sorry," what they really meant was, "I can't shut up."

Bob nudged me in the ribs. "Dude, the crayfish is tearing a hole in the box. What should we do?"

I glanced down at the Pabst box. Sure enough, a big-ass crayfish claw stuck out the bottom, but not wanting to be a hypocrite about the whole silence thing, I kept my mouth shut.

"Dude...*dude*," Bob said.

I remained stoic. Besides, I kind of figured that if the young women didn't find us so creepy, they probably would've asked for some form of comfort. Instead, they kept casting wary glances at Bob and me, as if we hadn't just called 911 in an effort to help. I couldn't blame them. We probably looked like a couple of whacked-out dudes with our massive sturgeon rods and an enormous crustacean attempting to break its way free of a Pabst Blue Ribbon box. Yeah, if I were them, I'd have been a little suspicious too. I started to laugh, thinking how humans could look upon other humans as alien. What a lonely species. But I stifled my laughter, because of the silence. *You fucking hypocrite*.

"*Dude*..." Bob was still trying. He whispered harshly. "Seriously man, I don't know why you're ignoring me, but you gotta take this crayfish. I need to piss. Bad. Like five minutes ago. Just take the box."

I took the beer box and Bob waddled over to some bushes to relieve himself. He was mid-piss when four police officers approached, two from each side of the Esplanade. There was perfect timing and there was this. They looked from Bob to me to the young women on the ledge, then back to

Bob, who continued pissing. "I'm sorry," he said. "Once I get going, I can't stop."

Three of the officers hurried down to the rocky bank to help the girls, while one remained behind to question us.

"Did one of you call this in?" the officer asked.

"It was his phone," I said, pointing at Bob.

"Sir, I'm going to ask you to stop peeing," the officer said to Bob.

"I told you..."

"Sir, I'm not going to ask again." The officer put a hand on his gun holster, as if pissing was a life-threatening offense.

Bob tucked his pecker back in his pants and zipped up. When he turned around to face me and the officer, a dark snake of urine streaked down his left pant leg to his ankle. "See what you made me do?" Bob said, but the officer wasn't listening.

"Is that a lobster?" the officer said.

"It's a crayfish," I said. "We caught it just a bit ago."

"You caught that thing *here*?"

"Sure did."

"Jesus. I didn't know they got that big."

"They don't," Bob said.

The paramedics arrived and carted off the young woman whose boyfriend had died. Her friends issued police statements and then hurried away, presumably to head to the hospital. The officer who told Bob to quit pissing and then expressed surprise at the giant crayfish remained behind to question us. The questions were routine and unenlightening for all parties, but I accepted the necessity of the procedure. Bob was a little less understanding. He fidgeted with his hands, fucked with the crayfish, removed a Pabst from his tackle bag only to be told by the officer that he couldn't drink that here. After running through the standard questions, the officer turned to walk away, but hesitated. "What're you going to do with that thing?" he asked, gesturing to the crayfish.

"We thought we'd call ODFW."

"That's probably a good idea," the officer said.

After he walked away, we stood there, looking out at the river, the lights of downtown Portland reflecting on the water.

"How come we didn't tell him about the river monster?" I asked.

"I don't know. I figured you'd mention it."

"Yeah, well I thought you'd mention it."

"Doesn't matter," Bob said. "He didn't ask."

"Yeah, but that girl's boyfriend was killed."

"So? They'll think she's hysterical. I mean, she is. Do you want to get roped in with all that shit? We're better off alone."

We looked at the crayfish as it broke its other claw through the cardboard box.

"It's gonna escape soon," I said.

"Yeah, probably will."

"So we gonna call ODFW now?"

Bob sighed heavily. "Man, I know I was acting strange around that cop. You have to understand. I don't like authority figures. I have what you call a disdain for them. Cops, doctors, politicians, judges, TSA, NSA, CIA...they're all assholes in my book. We should report this. It's wrong *not* to report what we've seen, but I can't do that, man. You can, if you want. Just don't involve me in it. I'll go away. I won't be around."

"Bob, what're you trying to say?"

"Before my time in Alaska, and a couple times since moving here, I've been hospitalized for like, shit that goes on in my brain. I have brain problems, Gordon. I don't really know what all goes on before I'm hospitalized. I never had any friends, so there's never anyone around to tell me what I'm being like. Then I go away. Or they come for me, I should say."

"Who comes for you?"

"The goddamn authorities."

"Are you on medication?"

"I was. I mean, I have been. I stopped taking it."

"And you're okay now, aren't you? Everything is fine?"

"I JUST DON'T LIKE COPS," Bob shouted. He was getting worked up, breathing hoarsely, balling his fists, his face reddening. "I'D KILL A COP WITH MY COCK IF I COULD GET IT UP. OR BASH HIS HEAD IN WITH A CUCKOO CLOCK." He cocked his arms into wings and flapped them violently. "Cuckoo. Cuckoo. Cuckoo."

A couple walking past gave Bob a wide berth. The homeless crisis in Portland bordered on epidemic, so anyone living in the city was well-acquainted with the erratic behavior not only of the homeless, but also the weirdo artist types who called Portland home. Still, I didn't know how to react. Passing a crazy on the street was one thing. Realizing that your new best friend might be crazy was something else entirely.

I stood there, feeling helpless and defenseless, as Bob went through the motions of some kind of breakdown.

The giant crayfish finally broke entirely free of its cardboard prison. Slowly, it backed away from us, claws raised in case anyone else decided to fuck with it. I watched it go, but the state of Bob left me too heartbroken and disarmed to act.

The crayfish scuttled down the Esplanade, returning the way we had walked, as if it knew where it was going, even on land, and home was calling.

I must have gotten distracted watching the crayfish walk away, the lights of the Esplanade reflecting off its deep red exoskeleton, because the next thing I knew, something large and heavy splashed into the river beyond the ledge and Bob was no longer freaking out next to me. Bob was nowhere to be seen. Then his head bobbed up in the dark current before he went under again. Out in the channel, a spiny dorsal fin as big as a parasail appeared, slicing through the water.

I ran to the ledge and looked on helplessly as the river monster surged toward the spot where Bob had gone under.

Bob surfaced, his chest and arms breaking above the water. He was doing the butterfly stroke. Despite the apparent oddity of it, he was making good headway toward the rocky bank. The gigantic dorsal fin vanished underwater.

My heart thudded in my chest. I wanted to jump in and drag my friend ashore, but I knew that could get us both killed. I wanted to scream, but my throat felt like it was full of steel wool.

Bob was ten feet from shore now.

So close.

A couple more strokes and he'd be on dry land.

He made it to the boulders and lifted himself up, but he slipped back into the water. His body spasmed in an unnatural way, as if something jerked him from beneath. He clung to a rock, the water up to his chest, as a boil appeared behind him, like a giant bass about to strike at prey.

The darkness that enveloped him did not take the form of a fish in my eyes. Not at first. I beheld a darkness so vast, so complete, that at first I thought the world was being swallowed up, as if a black hole had spontaneously developed and would now proceed to suck all the earth and more into its insatiable, infinite jaws. But the darkness had teeth. Jagged white triangles. They tore into Bob. Even in the low light, I could see the plumes of blood that mushroomed in the murky water like miniature atomic bombs. The blood was not what held my attention though. Not the blood or Bob's struggle with the river monster. All that faded into the background, the world turned quiet, as one of the horrible fish's eyes pinned me in its gaze. The eye was the size of a dinner plate and yellow like an alcoholic's piss. There was no pupil. The eye was all yellow. The fish paused its gnashing to study me. We held each other's gaze.

I couldn't help but feel I was being analyzed, broken down into raw data, but that was the sort of thing a machine would do, not a prehistoric fish.

For reasons I will never understand, the river

monster slunk back into the depths and swam off into the night.

Somehow I knew the creature would not attack again, and I scrambled down the ledge and dragged my mangled friend ashore.

Not long after, police arrived on boats with divers to search for the drowned man. I flagged them down and it was only thanks to their presence that Bob survived.

*

I sat in the waiting area of the ER, sipping scalded coffee from a Styrofoam cup. In my pocket rested a massive, shimmering-dark fish scale. Before the ambulance had arrived, Bob had tried to hand the fish scale to me. He had apparently torn it off the fish in the struggle. The scale dripped this viscous slime and I hadn't wanted to touch it, so I'd wrapped it in a napkin and stuffed it in my pocket. Although I still had a ton of questions and no answers concerning Bob's apparent psychotic break with reality, I understood the fish scale. With it, we could find out what we were up against. Well, what I was up against. Bob was in the ICU. When I dragged Bob out of the river, both of his legs were gone. The river monster was still out there, free to feast again.

The Man Who Went Blind Staring at the Moon

I fell asleep in the chair beside Bob's bed. I had a dream in the third person, like watching a movie, about a man who was neither Bob nor I, but in some indescribable way I knew in the dream -- and still know now -- that this man I dreamed of represented the secret, deepest part of Bob and myself. Then again, it's easy to get mixed up when you follow dreams. Doesn't matter what the dream means, really. I always dreamed of mundane things, so this stuck out, kind of showed me there was more to myself than I'll ever find out, especially now, so close to the end of the road. Anyway, here's that dream I had. It feels important.

*

For many nights, the man stared at the moon. He stood on the creaking Esplanade that floated over the dark river. A hundred feet below him, giant sturgeons lurked, while bats chased insects in the nighttime air. The city across the water cast a glow over the man, and occasionally a lone passerby asked him for a cigarette, but the man did not smoke, and he kept his eyes on the moon when he told them, "I don't smoke." Sometimes a sturgeon broke the surface, leaping entirely out of the water as if tempting the man to pry his eyes from the moon to take in its prehistoric form. The man never did, though. He kept his eyes on the moon all through the cold night. Only when the fog rolled in around sunrise, obscuring his view of the moon, did the man notice the geese cutting through the fog, furry brown nutria feeding on perch in the backwater, fishermen trolling the shipping channel for chinook, the bridges rising and descending to make way for the freight ships hauling pyramids of dirt upriver, the black and blue skeleton of the night dissolved in an endless gray. He closed his eyes, and he sighed.

He brought a stout fishing pole with him along with a bag of dough, and once the moon had gone away, he fished for carp so that he might have something to eat during the long, lonesome daylight hours, away from the moon. He'd catch a carp and take it to his little house and make a stew or bake the fish whole, or fry it up in batter, and then he'd sleep until the sun fell down and awaken and eat what remained of the carp and return to the river, where, like every night for as long as he cared to remember, he stood on the Esplanade and stared at the moon.

One particularly cold, wet night, the moon spoke to the man. Unfortunately, the moon spoke in a quiet voice, and its words were lost in the rainfall. The man held onto the lost words like gold. He imagined a whole host of things the moon might have said. He repeated those things so often to himself that eventually he believed the moon had said them all, when in fact what the moon said that night was anyone's guess.

The man believed that the moon told him he was a good person.

The man believed that the moon told him everything gets better.

The man believed that the moon told him don't be lonely.

The man believed that the moon said I love you.

You're a good person. Everything gets better. Don't be lonely. I love you.

On nights of the new moon, it was hard to believe the moon had ever said anything at all. The man pleaded with the moon to speak again. He prayed. He shouted. He cursed. He cried. Still the moon refused to listen. This tested the man's willpower. Why not climb over the railing of the Esplanade and gently slide into the river, sink down to live among the mysterious sturgeon, maybe become a sturgeon himself. But the man was not ready to drown, and he had no interest in becoming a sturgeon. All he wanted was to stare at the moon, to hear it speak. After many nights of staring at the moon, eventually the man went blind. Blindness is, was, and has always been the natural and inevitable fate of those who stare at the moon.

Here is how the man went blind.

When he arrived at the esplanade one evening, the man felt especially giddy. He sensed the moon this night would be special. The darkness came, and with it, the moon. And what a moon to behold, rising high above the glimmering city, like a million stars gathered in a net and mashed into a doughy round disc and baked in the oven of the night, rising, a pie made of light. This was the moon.

Once again, the moon spoke to the man, and it

said all the things he'd always believed it said on that rainy night so long ago.

"You're a good person.

"Everything gets better.

"Don't be lonely.

"I love you."

The man cried tears of joy as the moon spoke. His tears crystallized as they were squeezed from his eyes. They rolled down his cheeks and clattered against the Esplanade—little moon tears.

"Take me with you!" the man shouted, for even though shedding crystal tears made him feel closer to the moon, after so many nights alone and staring, the tears were not enough.

"I cannot take you with me," the moon said, "but here's what I can do."

The moon increased in brightness sevenfold, shining brighter than the man had ever seen it shine before. He opened his eyes wide, still shedding moon crystals, and let the brightness inside. He felt the moon's cold white hands embrace him. "You'll never be alone again," the moon said.

Then the moon was gone. The world was gone. The river, the bridges, the bats and the fish, the Esplanade beneath his feet – the man could see none of it anymore. I'm blind, he thought. He panicked momentarily, reaching up to feel his eyes, wondering if perhaps the moon crystals he cried somehow scratched his retinas, if the moon had tricked him somehow, but in each socket he felt a baseball-sized orb, a crater-pocked, powder-soft orb, rotating slowly in their sockets. The rain came down heavy and all at once, but in spite of the downpour, the man could hear two voices start to sing. "My eyes, my eyes," the man said, no longer afraid of his newfound blindness, realizing this was what he was after all along, this no longer being alone. He was filled with a white-hot glow that incinerated the gunk of loneliness, leaving behind nothing more than a pearl-white skeleton, miniature moons orbiting in his eye sockets, a smile on his fleshless mouth. The sun was coming up by about then, so the man went about his day.

Tonight There's Gonna Be a Jail Break

The river monster and the crayfish were just the beginning. A week after the river monster devoured Bob's sturgeon, it made its presence known to the entire city when it devoured a dozen competitors during the annual dragon boat racing competition. The monster destroyed two boats in a neck-and-neck race, chomping through their wooden dragon heads as if it thought they were real dragons. Then, it turned on the bodies flailing in water, swallowing some whole, leaving others to bleed to death. A few managed to swim to shore, but the damage had been done, recorded on smart phones by dozens of witnesses. Soon the whole world was watching, waiting for Portland's river monster to attack again. I watched the footage replay on the evening news in Bob's hospital room. Bob was so heavily medicated, he still fed through an IV and indicated thoughts with a meager thumbs up or thumbs down. I wasn't sure if the news was getting through to him or not, but I think he caught at least some of it.

The day after the tragic attack aired, I took the keys to Melinda and drove down to the Department of Fish and Wildlife's headquarters in Salem. I gave them the fish scale that Bob had pried from the monster and told them everything, all of it spilling forth in one long sentence. Our first encounter with the river monster, the giant crayfish, the killing of the young woman's boyfriend, then Bob being attacked.

Finally, the fish and game warden, who had unwrapped the napkin and picked up the fish scale, turning it between his fingers as I rambled on, cut me off. "Sir, we thank you for your information, but I'm going to ask you to leave the premises."

I was stunned. I tried to protest, but the warden stood up and pointed at the door. "Go. Now," he said in a stern voice.

Maybe Bob was crazy, but I wasn't, and footage of our river monster was broadcasting on televisions all across the country. The river monster was real.

I intended to hang around until ODFW filled me in on what was going on. I opened my mouth to say as much, but the warden cut me off before I could get a word in.

"I'm not fucking around," the warden said, standing up behind his desk. Then, before I could flee the office, the warden picked up his chair and smashed it against the window, shattering the glass. "I will not abide these bee stings on my mind!" the warden shouted. "You will not feed me chocolate pudding through a straw! I will not kill a dog!"

Several officers rushed in and restrained the warden, who fought them off and wielded the chair as a weapon. I fled during the commotion. I drove back to Portland, straight to the hospital. I tried calling the ODFW office but it went straight to the automated messaging system. That night I slept on a wheel-away cot beside Bob.

In the following weeks, the river attacks increased in frequency. Several fishing boats vanished. Sea lions all but vanished up near Oregon City. The only sign of them were the bloody sea lion heads and flippers that washed up on the beaches. A massive barge hauling pyramids of dirt to Ross Island was sunk. By the time the river patrol responded to the SOS call, the barge and its operators were gone. At that point, the city imposed a moratorium halting all activity, recreational and commercial, on the Willamette River.

Portland Harbor, the city's shipping port, shut down.

I watched the reports with increasing concern on the television in Bob's hospital room. As Bob's alertness increased, he watched the river monster reports too.

Everyone seemed to believe the giant fish caught on video was the only one of its type. There was no reason for the public to suspect otherwise. Without new footage of the monster, the nightly news reports aired interviews with average citizens about the situation. Most people seemed to believe the river monster should be hunted down and killed. Other than the river ban, the only statements issued by city, state, and federal bureaus were buried in politician jargon. They said a whole lot without saying anything at all, enlightening no one and offering no solutions. They promised nothing, as if the river monster were a major storm system that couldn't be stopped and not a predatory fish that could be hunted down and killed. Outrage intensified. Protests broke out, but so did the merchandise. Portland was already a big tourist town. People already visited from all over just to try

Voodoo Doughnut. Now people were visiting for a chance to witness the river monster.

Despite the increasing flurry of activity, the river monster had evaded the eye of the public since the dragon boat incident. Several shaky smart phone videos were posted online, but all turned out to be fakes.

Then, one day, the fish counter up at Willamette Falls saw something interesting. The coho run on the Willamette was unsubstantial and state budget cuts had slashed the fish counter's hours in half, so by the time they came to the odd footage, it was already three days old. They scanned the week's tape, recording coho, along with the occasional summer steelhead and chinook passing through the fish ladder. Everything was as usual until a cluster of what appeared to be lampreys appeared in the ladder. Confused over why the lampreys would be clustered together, the fish counter paused the video, counted out each individual lamprey in the mass, then let the footage roll again. The fish counter watched, first in confusion and then in horror, as the lamprey mass filled the fish ladder, blocking the passage to all other fish. As the lampreys moved up the ladder, the fish counter realized they were far too long to be lampreys. These weren't lampreys at all. They were black tentacles, twenty feet long at least. Before the head of the creature -- or whatever was attached to the tentacles -- appeared onscreen, the tentacles vacated the fish ladder and the creature slunk back into the river, as if it had only been curious where all the salmon were going. The fish counter called his boss on her cell phone. She was slightly annoyed to hear from him, until he told her what he'd just seen. Nobody was sure how the footage had leaked to KGW. The camera on the fish ladder at Willamette Falls couldn't be viewed online publicly like the fish ladder at Bonneville Dam. Ultimately, how the footage reached the public didn't matter. What mattered was that more than one river monster was lurking in the Willamette.

While this footage of the tentacles played on the news station for the thousandth time, Bob uttered his first coherent sentences since his psychotic episode. "So there's more than one of 'em," he said.

I nearly jumped out of my chair. I was so used to being alone in the room with Bob. Except for sporadic, incoherent statements, the way his vacant eyes fixated on the television screen during reports of the river monster, and the thumbs up/down system, he'd put forth few signs of actual consciousness.

"How do you feel?" I asked.

"Pretty swell for a double amputee," Bob said.

I was unsure whether that was supposed to be a joke or not. "Something strange is happening in the river," I said.

"Do you still have the fish scale I gave you?"

"I drove it down to ODFW's headquarters."

"And?"

"The warden flipped his shit, just like you did before you jumped in the river. Speaking of, I've been dying to ask you what the hell that was all about."

Bob nodded grimly. "I'm a liar, but whatever I said about my psychiatric history, that was probably all true. I've been through hell, man. Before the cops showed up down there, I started getting this itchiness in my veins, like my blood was on fire."

"If it counts for anything, I told the doctors that you fell in. I didn't tell them you were acting strange or anything."

"Thanks, buddy. And about that, I been thinking. I don't believe I was having one of my psychotic breaks. I think handling that crayfish did something to me. Drugged me. And you saying the warden freaked out after handling the fish scale...you didn't touch it, did you?"

I shook my head. "Hell no, that shit was slimy, and not normal fish slime either. I wrapped it in a napkin."

Bob looked relieved. "I'm glad you didn't touch it. I wanted to warn you, but I couldn't speak. Touching that crayfish did something to me. I thought I was having a psychotic episode. And I was. It was just induced by the crayfish. If the warden was acting crazy..."

"You think touching the fish scale did it?"

"I know it sounds insane, but I don't know what else to think."

"Then we're definitely up against something far worse than a giant muskie." I gestured to the looped footage of the tentacles squeezed into the fish ladder on the television screen. "And who knows how many of them are out there. They could turn the whole city crazy."

"Oh," Bob said, as if he didn't hear me. I couldn't blame him. He was probably still jacked up on pain medication. "Thanks for keeping the cops and reporters out of here. I couldn't have handled them busting down the door every day. It's been...peaceful."

"You don't have to thank me for that."

"I at least owe you a beer."

"No, you don't understand. Nobody's been by."

An expression of surprise crossed Bob's face. "Really?"

"Yeah, really."

"I figured because I'm a survivor of the river monster that they'd have some questions or something. I mean, they're interviewing random people off the street and we've actually seen the damn thing. Hell, it ate my legs."

"Yeah, man. I agree. It's fucking weird. If I owned the news station, I'd have a camera stationed in this room 24/7. I'd be reporting on your status morning and night. You'd be a legend. And the cops--"

"Fuck the cops. Fuck 'em all. I don't want to talk to them anyway." Bob tried to roll over on his side to face away from me, but he was stuck lying on his back. His face squinched up, his eyes pinched together, and he looked sort of like a prune. He started to cry.

"Oh, hey man, it's alright," I said. "The doctor's gonna talk to you about prosthetic options. With the advances that have been made in recent years, he says military-grade prosthetics are available to everyone. You'll be up and walking again in no time."

"It's not that," Bob said.

"Then what is it?"

"All my life I've been overlooked. When my big brother led the high school football team to the regional championship, it was a fucking holiday in our town. We practically had reporters living on our lawn. My parents took out a second mortgage on their house so they could buy my brother a new truck. We'd go out to eat as a family and his meal would be comped. The high school gave him his own parking spot. Everybody treated him like a god. Even after he tossed three interceptions that essentially sealed their fate and prevented them from advancing to the state championship, my brother was all that and a bag of potato chips. I can't blame them. He was everything to me too. Where other kids looked up to rock stars or pro athletes, I had my brother. Two years later, he's off to college and I'm a senior. They've finally given me a shot to fill his shoes. I'm the starting quarterback. And you know what I do?"

"You fucked everything up?"

"God, I almost wish I did. I shattered every school passing record and led us all the way to the state championship, which we won."

"Then what's the problem?"

"Nothing," Bob said. "Nothing is the problem. I wasn't celebrated by anyone. I never once received a game ball. Somehow the coaches always found someone who'd performed better, even in our 29-28 win over our town rival, in which I passed for three touchdowns, ran for another, *and* took in a two-point conversation on a quarterback sneak, driving home the win. I threw for seven touchdowns and five-hundred yards one night and the game ball went to the kicker. It was the best year of my life and also the worst. Nobody ever even told me good job. Not once. The local paper wrote a single article on my record-breaking season, but the reporter focused more on my brother, how he was the backup quarterback at Cal and really deserved a shot to start. My parents didn't even attend my games. My play didn't evade recruiters though, and I was sent around half a dozen offers to play college ball. I left each letter on my father's desk, hoping he'd take an interest. I was willing to go to college wherever made him happy. Problem was, *I* didn't make him happy. He refused to speak a word to me about football or college, and so when the deadline to commit to a college came and passed, I'd made a decision to quit football forever. Nobody missed me."

"Damn, man. That's shit luck."

"The universe finds me an absolute bore." Bob laughed grimly. "I don't know what it is I did in a previous life, but I must be the most uninteresting person on the planet. Nobody's ever cared about anything I've said or done except for Melinda, and she's an automobile. And now you. Thanks for that, man."

"I'm not sure what to say. Except fuck the world. You're not the boring one. They are."

"Yeah, I mean if being the lone survivor of a river monster can't get me on the news, then my aura definitely radiates total boredom."

"Well, technically you're not the only survivor. Some of the dragon boat racers made it back to shore."

"Did any of 'em lose any limbs?"

"Of the survivors? No."

"And were they on the news?"

"While you were sleeping this morning, they were on *Good Morning America*."

"Son of a bitch. I must be so fucking boring."

"You're not boring. You're just weird. These dragon boat racers were all young, pretty people."

"Was I weird when I was a high school quarterback?"

I imagined Bob in high school with his scraggly goatee, irregularly receding hairline, and bad teeth. "I bet you were weird back then too."

"You think they'll put me on the news if I get prosthetic legs with rocket boosters?"

"Stop trying to get on the damn news. It's stupid anyway, and it's advantageous to us if nobody cares about our weird asses."

Bob sulked. "How so?" he said, more a statement of defiance than a question.

"You know how many times a day the nurses come check on you?"

Bob shrugged.

"One time a day. Two if you're lucky. The doctor hasn't been by in a week. You've been wiped out on pain meds all this time, so you haven't noticed, but if it wasn't for me taking care of you, you probably would've rotted away in here."

"And that's supposed to make me feel better?" Bob said.

"It means we can break you outta this place any time we want and nobody will even notice. Trust me, I don't think you can afford the bill you've racked up in here."

"What about my prosthetics?"

"Oh man, I was just lying to make you feel better. You ain't getting no military-grade prosthetic legs." I pointed over to the corner. "That's your new legs, baby."

Over in the corner sat a wheelchair. I had blown a chunk of my savings on a decent model. I'd also quit my job, or been fired or whatever, but my apartment was cheap and I could afford to get by for another few months before money trouble caught up with me.

"Are you saying tonight there's gonna be a jail break?" Bob said.

"Oh yeah, brother," I said, nodding, "that's exactly what I'm saying."

The Unluckiest Man on Earth Counts His Blessings

Bob ripped his IV out of his arm and I lowered him into the wheelchair. I snatched up a couple extra packages of gauze and stuffed them in the undercarriage compartment of the wheelchair. I didn't want Bob's stumps to fester under old bandages.

I stepped out into the hall to ensure the coast was clear. The hospital wing appeared to be empty. I opened the door wide and Bob wheeled himself forward. He cut a clean ninety degree turn and sped down the empty hall toward the elevator.

We took the elevator to the parking level and found Melinda waiting for us. Bob teared up again at the sight of her. "I'll never drive her again," he said.

"You'll be fine, man." I tried to help Bob out of his wheelchair into the passenger seat, but Bob slapped me away.

"You don't understand. Her pedals are like her clitoris. My feet are my dick. How the hell can I stimulate her if I've got no legs?"

"She's an automobile. Whether you're driving or I'm driving doesn't matter to her."

"Whatever will get her rocks off," Bob muttered, then he shouted at the Land Rover: "Isn't that right, Melinda? You Cockney slut."

I wasn't sure what a Cockney slut was and I doubted Bob knew either, but the shouting was drawing the attention of other people in the parking garage, so I lifted Bob up and hauled him into the passenger seat. The wheelchair folded up nice and compact. I tossed it in the back and hopped into the driver seat. Bob sat curled against the passenger-side door, mumbling to himself. Before we did anything else, we needed to score some painkillers. With the heroic doses the hospital had been pumping into Bob, he'd be experiencing withdrawals within hours.

Luckily, my upstairs neighbor dealt Oxys.

We pulled out of the hospital parking garage, paying an outrageous parking fee on the way out, and headed down toward Burnside Bridge.

*

Except for the quick trip to Salem, I had not been outside since knowledge of the river monster -- now river *monsters* -- became widespread knowledge. I'd seen footage of protesters and crowds hopeful to catch a glimpse lined up along the high sea wall on the west side of the waterfront park, but the news segments failed to prepare me for the chaos I was seeing now. Burnside Bridge was shut down to a single lane. Cars going either direction had to take turns crossing the bridge without a traffic cop to direct them. The crowds of people and wandering street vendors made the passage nearly impossible. People pressed up against the sides of the bridge, taking photos and staring down into the murky water a hundred or so feet below. When they'd grown bored of seeing nothing, they wandered into the masses and others filled their bridge-side spot. The setting sun glinted off Mt. Hood, which towered in the distance, but nobody looked at the mountain or the sunset. Their heads remained lowered to the river, or fixated on the beer and ice cream and street food they were consuming. I was pretty sure I spotted a tallboy of some craft beer sporting the illustrated likeness of the river monster on the can. There was even a balloon man making river monsters for the children. It was like the waterfront carnival had moved up onto Burnside Bridge, except down in the waterfront park, the crowds appeared even thicker. The river monsters had turned Portland into a big parade.

Bob and I inched along in Melinda, looking aghast at what we saw.

Finally, the crowd grew thinner as we crept onto lower West Burnside, where the homeless lined both sides of the street, some of them lying on sleeping bags and cardboard, others hanging out, drinking and smoking.

"Hey, I used to live there," Bob said, pointing to a semi-permanent homeless encampment outside the entrance to Chinatown. "Those guys were chill. I liked living there."

The encampment occupied an empty lot. It was walled in by a fence of colorfully painted doors that had been nailed together. There was an entrance on one side with a resident posted to monitor who came and went at all hours. A number of years back, I recalled reading about the real estate developers who owned the lot trying to evict the encampment, but evidently that had failed, as the encampment remained.

"You're not homeless now, are you, Bob?" I asked.

"No, I rent a room in Lents. Can't say I spend much time there, but I need an address to collect my disability checks. Otherwise I'm happy enough sleeping in the back of Melinda."

"You need to run by there at some point?"

"I doubt I'll be running anywhere any time soon."

"Shit, I'm sorry. I meant--"

"I'm just messing with you. I know what you meant. And yeah, I should probably stop by. I was probably evicted for not paying rent, but what can I do? I was in the hospital. At least I can collect my mail."

"I should've taken care of that stuff for you."

"Naw, you didn't know."

"And what about your job? You mentioned work before."

"Oh, I volunteer in a soup kitchen. I'm sure they're worried about me, but it's no big deal. I've disappeared on them before."

"How long were you homeless?"

"Until four years ago. So let's see...I guess that means I was homeless for around five years."

"Jesus."

"It wasn't always so bad. That place back there, I had a bed and access to a shower. It's a drug-free zone too, so you're not around addicts like some of the other shelters, or sleeping downtown."

I thought of the people who sometimes slept in the alcove outside my apartment. I wondered if one of those people had ever been Bob.

"I slept in Melinda about eighty percent of that time too."

"I'm surprised you'd sleep apart for any of it."

"She was stolen, Gordon. It was a terrible year for both of us."

"Damn, and you recovered her in good condition? I bet you counted your lucky stars that day."

"I was walking down Southeast 82nd one day when I saw her on the lot of a used car dealership, one of those real shady places that promises low financing with zero down-payment to everyone. I'd just happened to collect my first disability check that day, so I walked in and bought her under a fake name, with a fake driver's license and an out-of-state address. I made a down-payment of $300 and signed a criminally-bad lease. I drove off the lot with her, and those sons of bitches never received another dime from me. They could never track me down in a million years."

"That's completely insane, but I respect your balls."

"Huh, yeah, I got big balls," Bob said.

"Fuckin' huge cojones."

"Alright, that's enough talk about my balls."

"Just saying. Sometimes I think I've been through the shit, that I've lived a hard life. You're giving me a whole new perspective on what the shit means. I mean, damn, you lost both your legs and you're acting as if everything is fine. And it's not only that. Life has pretty much dealt you a bad hand every time around. Most guys at least have a woman or a dog who's there for them when the chips are down, and you, all you got is a Land

Rover."

"That's not all I got," Bob said. "I got a friend in you now. Really, all I ever wanted out of life was a friend like you. Even when the crayfish turned me crazy or whatever, and I was out of my mind and I jumped into the river, even then I knew I was lucky. I always felt lucky though, even if I'm probably the unluckiest man on earth. I mean, hell, my brother was a thousand times more popular than me, but you wanna know where he ended up? He's dead. His sophomore year in college, he wrapped his truck, that nice new truck my parents bought for him, around a telephone pole while driving back shit-face drunk from a frat party. I've got my share of DUIs, but hey, I'm still kicking. Or flipping. Whatever you do with stumps. In my eyes, that makes me lucky, even if it means I'm not."

We pulled up to the curb outside my apartment. "You should crash at my place for a while," I said. "I quit my job, so who knows, I might need a roommate."

"I'd like that very much," Bob said.

Once we were settled inside, we opened a couple beers and I called in a pizza for delivery. I popped upstairs and picked up some Oxys from my neighbor, just in case Bob ended up in pain or the withdrawals got too bad, but he claimed to be feeling fine, tossed the pills aside and appeared to forget about them. That night, we drank beer, ate pizza, and poured over my collection of fishing books, seeking any information that might help us understand what was going on in the Willamette. We didn't find much that was useful, but we had a great time talking about fishing and sharing stories of past catches and observations on the water.

We sketched diagrams of what we knew so far. Giant muskie-like fish, jumbo crayfish, and ungodly tentacles.

"I think I've got it," Bob said, "I know what's really going on."

"What is it?" I asked.

"The Willamette has become a breeding ground for fucked-up shit."

"No shit, Sherlock. The question is, did pollution cause it, or did a portal to Hell open up?"

"Since I don't believe in Hell, I'd say pollution."

"Well, since the government doesn't believe in pollution, I guess they'd say Hell."

We burst out laughing even though the joke wasn't that funny or even a joke at all. We were just weird and drunk.

Only as I was climbing into my loft bed that night did I realize I hadn't checked my online dating profile in weeks. I paused on the ladder, debated going back down and turning on the computer. I was a little drunk, for one, and I wasn't getting any younger. My window of opportunity to find someone to settle down with felt like it was shrinking by the day. But then I realized that I *was* settling down. Becoming myself. Maybe I'd never have the life I envisioned for myself, with a wife and kids and a house with a big backyard, but I had this life. I could rest easy knowing that. I climbed into bed, feeling like the luckiest person on the planet.

*

The nightmare came through on the television. Hundreds dead or missing. Burnside Bridge had been destroyed. The black tentacles tore apart the bridge like a whole lot of Lego blocks. People tumbled down among the rubble into the dark water. Many drowned. Most were devoured by river monsters identical to the one that took Bob's legs. There were dozens of the monstrous fish, each twenty feet long, swift and savage.

Simultaneously, thousands of giant crayfish emerged on the beach south of Hawthorne Bridge and proceeded to crawl toward downtown. Two drunk bros were the first of their victims. The dudes filmed the slow invasion on their iPhones, but they underestimated the speed of the crustaceans and got too close. One of the dudes was taken down first, dragged into a pile of furious claws. His friend continued filming his death as he screamed through the agonizing process of being torn apart. The dude who couldn't bother helping out his friend never turned up at his girlfriend's apartment, where he was headed, but before he disappeared, he uploaded the footage of his friend being torn apart by crayfish to Facebook. Bob and I saw this video and more on the television as we sat there in my apartment, dumbfounded and in shock by what the news showed us. A wailing emergency siren had woken us. The siren was constant, deafening. We'd turned on the news because we didn't know what else to do. It wasn't even six in the morning. The governor of Oregon had declared a state of emergency in

Portland.

I had only felt this way once before in my life, and that was when I turned on the television on the morning of September 11th, 2001. The only difference was proximity. This nightmare was unfolding just over a mile away.

"Is this the end of the world?" I asked.

"It appears to be that way."

"Fuck my life."

Stunned by the unfolding reports, we drank beer with our breakfast instead of coffee. Within hours, thousands of Portland residents clogged the highways, attempting to flee north to Washington, south to Salem, west to the coast, or east to Hood River. We remained glued to the television. The National Guard was currently in a standoff with the crayfish on Southwest 10th, only eight blocks from my apartment. The crayfish were thick all the way down to the river, but at this point the National Guard appeared to have effectively contained them and news reports projected that the crayfish would be eliminated within the hour. Downtown residents were on lockdown, with no one allowed out of any residences until further notice. The black tentacles sank back into the dark water after the destruction of Burnside Bridge and had not been seen since. The fish had also vanished.

"Since we discovered the first one, what're we gonna name it?" I asked.

"What do you mean?"

"I mean, those things aren't muskies, and they sure as hell aren't anything else that ever existed before, so what do we call them?"

"I'll have to think on that one," Bob said.

"In South Africa, there were these fish called musselcrackers. Sometimes I'd be out fishing for rockfish, catching plenty of good edibles. I'd have a decent rockfish on the line, and as I'd be fighting it up, a big darkness would rise up and swallow my fish, and then I was in for a battle with a musselcracker. They usually broke me off or let go of the rockfish, but once in a while I'd haul one in. We're talking beastly fish. Fifty pounds, with jaws like vises..."

"And?"

"Oh, I don't know. I got to thinking about musselcrackers."

Bob slapped his bandaged leg stumps. "Why don't we just call them nightmare fish? I mean, that's what they are, the bloodthirsty bastards."

"Blood! That's it. We'll call them blood bass."

Bob squinted his eyes like he did when he was thinking deeply, mulling over the name. "Blood bass," he said. "Yeah, I like that. It's got a nice ring to it. Blood bass. Now if only we could catch one."

"Once a thing is named, you have power over it," I said.

"We gonna stroll down to the river and call 'em over? Maybe name each one individually? Come on, man. You said it yourself. We're fucked."

"Look, I know it's hopeless, but we need something here. Blood bass is something."

"Yeah, I guess it is." Bob laughed a little. "Blood bass."

A breaking news segment cut in on the television. The I-5 bridge that spanned the Columbia River, connecting the outskirts of Portland to Vancouver, Washington, was currently being wrenched from its moors by the black tentacles. The Willamette met with the Columbia only ten miles north of downtown Portland, so apparently the tentacled creature -- whatever it was -- had headed north after destroying Burnside Bridge. And now it was doing the same to the congested interstate bridge.

"Holy shit," Bob said.

"Is it me, or do those tentacles grow substantially every time we get a look at them?"

"They're definitely growing. Either that or they're different creatures, like the blood bass."

We watched the live footage, filmed from news helicopters, as the black tentacles coiled around the bridge like a serpent, but before the bridge collapsed, the tentacles reached out and slapped the helicopters out of the sky, one after the other, until all the news stations reverted back to in-station broadcasters looking confused and alarmed. Without further warning, television broadcasts cut out entirely. And then so did the power.

The Many Mouths of Hell

One year later

The Great Goddess Melinda

That day in my apartment, when the power went out as Bob and I watched the black tentacles tyrannize our city on live television, marked the end of our friendship. I'm not saying we parted ways right then. We remained each other's best and only friend. But the end of civilization changed Bob in strange and unexpected ways, and civilization most certainly took a nosedive toward extinction on that day. Even though Melinda sat outside, we remained in my apartment for a full week after the power went out. As we'd seen on television, the highways were closed. There was nowhere to go. Maybe things got better, but we had no interest in taking the risk, at least not until the beer in my fridge ran out. Looters also posed a problem. Between them and the crayfish, which persisted in unfathomable droves, the National Guard had their hands full. The violence spread all the way up to Southwest 18th, right outside my apartment. Fortunately, the apartment building looked like a rundown office complex and nobody ever tried to break in. As a precaution, I'd dug my hunting rifles out of the closet. Bob and I each slept beside one. That week was the longest of my life. I'd like to think of it as hell, but in truth, that time was awesome. Bob and I broke out my collection of barley wines, some of them aged up to five years, and we had ourselves a good time. A quiet time. We didn't want to alert anyone to our presence. It's amazing to think of that time as only lasting a week. I swear, it felt more like a year. But when the beer ran out, we grew restless. We couldn't last long in solitude and silence without beer. We decided to risk it. We crept out around dawn, late enough that we wouldn't have to rely on Melinda's headlights to guide us, but early enough that we still had the cover of dark. What were we looking for? I don't know. Bob told me where to turn, as if some GPS system in his heart directed him exactly where to go. I should've known. He led me to the homeless encampment on Burnside, the one he said he'd lived in for a while. Luckily they recognized Bob because otherwise I think they would've eaten us. Instead, they welcomed us in. They'd already raided nearby corner markets for cigarettes and were well stocked on Camels and Pall Malls, so I was inclined to stick around, at least for the free cigarettes.

You might wonder how civilization collapsed so quickly. After all, most of the city was still intact. The thing is, societies like ours, so steadfast, so secure, exist on the brink of chaos. The wrong wind blows and we fall in. The problem here was that Portland lacked the infrastructure to handle such a crisis. Hell, the city shut down every time it snowed. Introduce an unexpected element like, say, towering black tentacles, ravenous blood bass, and killer crayfish, and you'll soon find that all first world systems unravel. Our system of checks and balances, paperwork and audits, caves under the pressure. Even the National Guard sort of just left after a while. I don't know if they were called out or walked out against orders. All I know is one day we were left alone to defend ourselves against the crayfish, which thankfully only crept out of the river during rainstorms and at night. And luckily the homeless encampment was secure, like a bunker, so we felt pretty well-off, all things considered.

The other thing about a crisis is that rational thinking flies out the window. Looking back, we had so many opportunities to escape, or attempt escape, but the madness of our lives had infected us, altered our brains, like those soldiers who voluntarily return to war zones time after time, addicted to war. Like that, we became addicted to the end of the world. I would have left, I'm sure, if Bob would have agreed to it, but the times changed Bob. I barely knew him, and yet I'd lost my only friend, so I clung on, desperate to get him back from whatever darkness was eating him. I'll get to that shortly. In a way, he's my reason for writing all of this.

Rumors started spreading about black tentacles in other cities. We never had any means of verifying the truth of these reports because we were cut off from the outside world, so the rumors remained only hearsay. If you're reading this, maybe you know whether they were true or not. For your sake, I hope we were the only ones.

So there we were, one week into the apocalypse, I guess what you might call our voluntary apocalypse, since we could've presumably left it behind at any moment if we weren't so fucking crazy, and we go from my apartment to this homeless encampment, which is now maybe the safest place in the city because the shitheads in the high-rises and the suburbs all tore each other apart.

Like I said, crazy times breed crazies. Those people weren't even anywhere near the river. It still shocked me how quickly things collapsed, as if everybody in the whole goddamn city was just waiting to turn on one another. Ultimately, the river monsters were a catalyst for collapse, not the source of collapse. Thinking of everything that has come to pass, I can hardly believe it, but it happened, so what can I do? I'll be dead soon.

Bob and all the folks who populated the encampment, they responded differently to the stimulus of the end of the world. They had no interest in tearing one another apart. In fact, the downfall of society was like an opportunity to them. They'd lived in ruins for decades. Now that the whole city was in ruins, they believed it was their time to rise up, recruit, and take over. They'd thrived for so long in misery and squalor, they knew how to carve out a happy life under the worst conditions. So what did they do? The more important question is, what did Bob do?

He became an emissary to the gods.

That's what he did.

He'd been amassing this cult for a decade or more, making friends, telling lies about his history, until the stars aligned for him to bring all his best friends together into one big Bob-worshiping family.

And he somehow convinced everyone, including me, to worship Melinda, his only begotten Land Rover.

And in a culture where cars are status symbols, perhaps it wasn't much of a stretch to view one as a religious symbol.

It was creepy, I agree. But Bob was creepy in those days. Like I said, our apocalypse changed him.

And don't even ask what our ceremonial rites in worship of Melinda looked like, unless you want to imagine a bunch of dirty naked dudes in a big circle-jerk, masturbating one after the other into the gas tank of a car. I'm not saying that's what we did. All I'm saying is someone was working a miracle, because Melinda's fuel mileage turned incredible, like hybrid car good.

But worshiping Melinda, his only begotten Land Rover, was not what turned Bob into an emissary to the gods. The Melinda worship was a subsidiary distraction more than anything. I think Bob just wanted other people to feel as strongly about his vehicle as he did, maybe because he felt psychologically crippled, being unable to pleasure Melinda by driving her like he used to. Anyway, for other reasons, unexplainable reasons, we agreed to stand in as her husbands.

Mostly, we all loved Bob.

Why?

Because we were lonely. Not as lonely as he was, but in his depths of loneliness we saw ourselves reflected. Because basically everybody was Bob's best friend the way I was his best friend. The encampment was full of all the people who had played the role of Bob's best friend before me. I was one of many. He'd lied when he said I was the best and only friend he ever had. And basically, he asked me to fall back in line, to find my place in his congregation, and I did, for the same reason all the others did, because we all secretly hoped that Bob might still someday call us up from the ranks to become his best friend again.

There was another reason we went along with it too.

Remember me talking about drugs?

Yeah, we found a new drug, a better drug, and if we wanted our fix, we had to do whatever Bob said.

Let me tell you about black slime.

How Soon is Never?

The dark sky is bluing on the horizon, like a bruise. They'll come for me at dawn, for the ritual. There's so much left to tell, but time is limited. I can only put down the bare essentials and a stern warning to never smoke the black slime. The changes that are occurring within myself...the scales growing upon my back...even if I had not been chosen by Bob to be the next sacrifice, I would likely kill myself to avoid the cruel and inevitable fate wrought upon me by the black slime. Either that or lose myself in the substance, in hopes of burying my ego and ceasing to be Gordon West all together, forever, and slinking into the river, to lurk in the depths with my fallen brethren. I hope it's not too late for you.

As the encampment expanded its borders, amassing resources and more cult members to worship at the altar of Melinda, Bob's ambition also broadened. He began looking to the river. He wanted to cease control of West Burnside all the way down to the destroyed bridge. He kept his thoughts to himself, sharing nothing with his congregation, but the way he gazed upon the river, I knew he wasn't finished with the blood bass yet. The crippled king of the wasteland was plotting his revenge.

If we'd already tumbled down a rabbit hole, then we were about to fall into a viper pit far deeper, far darker, than anything we had previously been capable of knowing.

Order of the Black Tentacle

Turns out we weren't the only cult holding out in the Portland apocalypse.

We learned to move among the crayfish at night, mostly through staying close to structure, avoiding being out in the open. Bob wanted us to extend our territory down to the river. We lacked the resources to construct a physical barrier walling off Chinatown and the lower southwest, so in order to protect the territory from the occasional looter, photographer, or wanderer, we established patrol squads. There were about fifty of us in the camp, so patrols were divided up into rotating teams of ten men. I never asked the name of anyone I patrolled with and they never asked mine. We crept from bar to bar, ransacking the liquor cabinets and collecting whatever food hadn't gone to the rats and roaches.

Somewhere along the way, Bob had come into the possession of a bunch of spray paint. He ordered us to tag this symbol -- a large, barbed fish hook -- on the doors, windows, and walls of every establishment we entered. Beyond the worship of Melinda and our total subservience to Bob, it wasn't yet clear what type of cult we were, at least to me. Ultimately, it hardly mattered. Bob ensured that we all had beds and access to water, food to eat and liquor to drink, and then there was the silent time. Every week, we each got five minutes alone with Bob. The only rule was that speaking was forbidden. You'd sit there with Bob, maybe holding hands, maybe closing your eyes, and you'd meditate, or at least pretend to meditate. I don't know what Bob was on about. All I wanted was my friend back, and the only way I knew how to do that was to go along with what he asked, which meant roving around in the darkness, tagging buildings with fish hook graffiti.

That's exactly what I was doing the night we encountered The Spy. I'm not sure what his name was because we killed him before we found out, but not before he told us about the Order of the Black Tentacle. Turns out, according to this dude who we captured, tortured, and killed, that a group of white collar occultists operating out of one of the wealthiest high-rises in the city were responsible for bringing about the river monsters. Our nameless victim, who claimed to be a member of this esoteric order, spilled the beans in exchange for a promise of sanctity, but that didn't stop Bob from personally slitting his throat and then ordering us to roast the dude over an open fire after he'd revealed all his secrets.

Yeah, we ate the guy. So what?

It's cannibalism, sure, but it's also the end of the world, and I was forced into it. Not to mention, if you're reading this, you've probably done the same, or worse. Nobody's a saint in the cult of Bob.

So our nameless prisoner, he told us how he and other members of significant wealth were individually approached by a self-styled entrepreneur who claimed to have made his money coding weaponry software for private military contractors. This entrepreneur had legally changed his name to Ubermensch. I'm going to refer to him as Ub because, for starters, I never knew the dude, and for two, what a shitbag thing to do.

Ubermensch.

Thing was, Ub knew his shit. He sought out people for what he promised would be the greatest investment of their lives: the end of the world. Ultimately, it amounted to little more than our own sad little cult, except we lived in a former homeless encampment and they lived in luxury condos, bathed in champagne, and wiped their asses with silk scarves.

It was well-known that the CIA and other federal agencies had explored the viability of occult practices. What was less known was that the military had not only maintained, but actually ramped up such activities in the twenty-first century. Through a military contact, Ubermensch had been handed the keys to the greatest occult-biological weapon of all kind: a portal to another dimension that happened to be buried beneath Portland Harbor. In fact, Portland Harbor got so polluted in the first place as a means to keep the portal closed. Attempts to clean up the superfund site never went anywhere because at the highest level of government, officials knew that dredging the Harbor posed the risk of opening the portal again. Turns out, there were other ways to open it, and Ub was eager to exercise them.

Ub reached out to approximately fifty bankers, investors, CEOs, and others in positions of power. According to our nameless resource, they'd rent out wine bars and fine restaurants for their initial meetings. Nobody understood what Ub was going on about at that point, but his promises of unfathomable power kept everybody hooked. Besides, he was footing the bill for all these extravagant meetings, and many of the prospective cultists knew each other from previous ventures, so there was the added bonus of fraternizing with wealthy colleagues and networking.

The first time Ub asked them to meet him in an abandoned pesticide factory on the river at a quarter past midnight, nobody questioned it. After all, when had the wealthy led the wealthy astray? Some of them stifled laughs when they showed up and Ub distributed dark robes and ancient prayer books that appeared to be bound in some type of pale flesh, but Ub had also brought along a substantial quantity of a particularly fine vintage cabernet, so nobody protested. They put on their hooded robes and got tipsy on wine. When Ub asked them to congregate on the decaying pier, they shuffled out of the abandoned factory.

The nameless provider of this information claimed that they were all very surprised and alarmed when Ub revealed a young woman, shackled with heavy chains and duct tape over her mouth. But when Ub asked them to turn to a page in the flesh-bound books he'd distributed, they opened their books and recited the occult incantation after him. It turned out the bound woman was a virgin sacrifice. At the end of the prayer, Ub stabbed her in the heart with a dagger that twisted and writhed like a living tentacle. Apparently she bled black, which had something to do with the tentacle-dagger, though even our source of knowledge wasn't too sure. He never saw the tentacle-dagger again. Ub cast the woman into the river, which was almost too much for this group of millionaires-turned-occultists, but after the roiling current swept her under, Ub commanded them to proceed with the festivities. As if under hypnosis, they communally shrugged off the virginal sacrifice and proceeded to get hammered on the particularly fine vintage cabernet. In the morning, our informant claimed, they hardly remembered a thing about the previous night, except that maybe some young woman had gotten too drunk and fallen into the river.

The following week, Ub gathered his unwitting cult once again at the abandoned pesticide factory. Some of them were growing impatient, but Ub promised to reveal the seeds of their future power at this meeting. Once again, there were dark-hooded robes and fleshy prayer books, good wine and a virgin to be sacrificed. There was no weird dagger this time. Instead, when Ub called them all out to the pier, he pitched the shackled sacrificial virgin into the river without stabbing her at all. Once again, there was nearly a voice of protest, but before anyone could say that maybe murder wasn't what they had in mind when they signed up for this, a great river monster -- what Bob and I named a blood bass -- exploded on the river's surface, chowing down on the shackled woman almost as quickly as she'd hit the water. The nameless source of this information had another name for the blood bass, but I like blood bass better. You don't need to know the other name. It's not important.

Now, at this point, apparently there was quite a furor. Human sacrifices were one thing. River monsters turned out to be quite another.

Ub utilized all his creepy mind-control techniques to remain in command of the situation. He managed to convince everyone that if they'd just open their prayer books and recite a particular incantation along with him, then all would be revealed. Their mindless cooperation was our source's first indication that perhaps the excellent vintage wines they'd been imbibing might've contained a little something extra, but he'd consumed his fair share and opened his book to the proper incantation like the rest, despite this dawning realization that they were all being drugged.

Upon this recitation, which we were told was far too unspeakably hideous to repeat, lest we also become infected by its cadences, a blood bass rose up and devoured the sacrificial woman, but something else happened soon after. The black tentacles, that by this time I knew too well, also emerged from the river.

Ub stood on the edge of the pier and raised a pewter bowl to the dark sky. He shouted lines that did not appear in the prayer while everybody else stood around, under the spell of a strange drug, likely screaming inside but unable to sync up their bodies with their minds. The black tentacles lowered themselves like the heads of a hydra over Ub. They juiced a thick dark fluid into the pewter bowl.

The bowl filled, the tentacles returned to the river. Ub drank from the bowl, then passed it around to the cultists, who partook of the dark fluid. The consistency was somewhere between a liquid and a jelly. It blackened their mouths like octopus ink. Not a single soul who was present that night showed up for work the next day. They left their families and their powerful jobs behind. From that day forward, they lived for the black slime.

Our nameless prisoner from this other cult, which eventually came to calling itself Order of the Black Tentacle, described the effects of this drug as being something akin to total sensory deprivation. All sight, sound, smell...the whole world basically...everything dissolves into what he called "the carbonated night." From there, he claimed, shit got real, and he couldn't speak about the black slime anymore because even the thought of its effects forced his face into a grin so wide, his mouth bled a little at the corners.

We thought he was crazy, but the allure of a new drug with perception-shattering effects was too great a temptation for Bob. He had to find out for himself, and he did. We all did.

From firsthand experience, I can tell you that our prisoner was no liar. Even though we had to resort to torture to extract most of this information from him.

When pressured to spill the present whereabouts of Ub and the Order of the Black Tentacle, our prisoner told us that the cult had splintered. Apparently, Ub's initial plan involved acquiring the black slime for resale. A brand new drug, so otherworldly that its effects defied human language. It was a drug that defied earthly chemistry. Despite the occult theatrics, the hooded robes and flesh-bound books, not to mention the stupid name, crass capitalism coursed through Ub's blood. At his heart, he was a businessman. He'd been led down this path by greed, boredom, and a desire to watch the elite citizens of an American city prostrate themselves in the pursuit of greater profit and power. Everything was going according to plan. Once everyone had sipped from the bowl of black slime, the consecration was complete. And Ub, as their link to the bizarre creatures that had been summoned from the portal in the river, was in total control. The ground floor of his new empire was complete. It could've worked out too, if black slime wasn't so addictive.

By the time we came to hear all this, apparently the Order of the Black Tentacle had already splintered into warring factions. Our prisoner said it wasn't much of a war because all the sides were too drug-sick to effectively carry out war strategies. At least half of them had turned into fish people and slunk into the river, only ever seen if an opportunity for a human feast presented itself. However, a screwdriver through the meat of his hand expelled some new information from our resource. He said the factions had abandoned downtown and migrated south. Some of them lived in the forest near the riverfront amusement park on the east side. Those who retained some memory of their former wealth moved into the empty high-rises that lined the western waterfront. He said he'd been sent downtown from one of these factions because rumors of our little cult had spread. The black tentacles continued providing black slime to all those who offered up human sacrifices, but it was getting difficult to lure members of other factions into booby traps. His faction got the idea that if they could somehow capture an entire unwitting group of a few dozen or more people all at once, they'd have a veritable farm of sacrificial lambs. If they strung us along for long enough, they could even breed us with the handful of women in our camp, and thereby raise sacrifices forever, and never run out of black slime again. If turning into a fish person sounds bad, he told us, then you don't even want to know what black slime withdrawals are like.

Soon, our nameless prisoner began to show these symptoms of withdrawal, and he was right about it being so much worse than turning into a fish. Crayfish tore through his chest cavity and attacked us. We set them on fire with torches and saved the man's carcass from the flames. This was also how we learned that black slime withdrawals were responsible for the population of giant crayfish. Once the drug left your system, your blood started crystallizing into small crayfish that would grow exponentially unless you consumed black slime. Those without a supply of the drug on hand were wrenched apart from the insides by thousands of crayfish that had formed from their blood. Once we became addicted to black slime ourselves, some in our encampment also died this way. We set them on fire, each and every one.

That is more or less all I know about the Order of the Black Tentacle. They are responsible for the end of Portland, possibly the world, and consequently, for the end of my friendship with Bob, which was so far gone by this point I'd given up hope of ever repairing what we had, even though I still loved him, and I mourned for those too-few days we had together. But our crippled king had a new objective. He wanted black slime, and we who worshiped him were all too willing to deliver it.

Bobber Fishing

One day, Bob asked us for two things. He asked us to construct a gigantic fishing bobber and to paint it red and white, like the ones all fishermen use, especially when they are young. He said that the bobber ought to stay afloat while supporting up to three-hundred pounds of weight. Secondly, he asked us to fashion a fish hook the size of a human arm. Separate teams were sent out to salvage the parts and machines needed to devise this hook and bobber setup.

Fortunately, as I was never much of a craftsman myself, and perhaps because Bob still favored me in some way, even though he never showed it, I was given a separate task: acquire several thousand yards of the strongest fishing line available. Ordinarily, that would require crossing the bridge to Ollie Damon's but Burnside Bridge had been demolished. It didn't take much thinking to realize that Bob had assigned me to find fishing line because he knew my apartment was full of the stuff, so that night, I set out walking up West Burnside, back to my old apartment, which I hadn't visited since Bob and I left after the first period of the apocalypse, which I'd rank up there among the very best days of my life.

When I walked in the door, tears welled in my eyes and I broke down crying on the cold tile floor. I couldn't believe all I'd gone through, all I'd endured for the sake of Bob. "Why? Why did you do this to me?" I shouted, not caring who heard me, if there was even anyone left to hear me.

I decided not to return to the encampment. I'd resume residence in my apartment. Fuck Bob and his cult of Melinda. I was done worshiping that fucking dude and his Land Rover. My apartment was only one step above the homeless encampment on the squalor meter, but at least it was my squalor. At least there I could live a life I could call my own. I even found a bottle of a bourbon barrel-aged stout that I'd stashed away in a cabinet some years ago. I opened it and made a toast to myself, to the first day of the rest of my life.

When it got dark that night, I sort of expected someone from the encampment to come for me. I figured Bob would send a mob to bring me back, but nobody ever came. The cupboards and fridge were empty, so the stout was my dinner that night. I found the bag of Oxys I'd bought from my neighbor so long ago. I took a couple of those for dessert. That night, I slept well.

Since Bob's crew tended to run the streets mostly at night unless on special errands, I took advantage of the day to scavenge for food. I already knew the big grocery store on West Burnside had been looted, but the British pub up in Goose Hollow remained unscathed. I filled a satchel with sardine cans and a bottle of whiskey. Cockroaches had devoured all the grains.

At home, I had the first of many sardine and whiskey feasts. I popped the rest of the Oxys. I passed out before sundown and awoke in the middle of the night, drenched in sweat, flashlights beaming through my canary yellow curtain. Someone pounded on the door. I tried to get up, but my limbs failed to function.

They'd come for me, like I knew they would.

And somehow, I was fine with that.

They beat me for no reason. Cracked a rib. Broke a tooth. They tied me up with rope. They rummaged through my shit and found the big-game strength fishing line I was supposed to bring back before I went AWOL.

Back at camp, they threw me in a prison cell, which was actually the shower stall with an appointed guard. But they untied me, and they gave me paper and a pencil, which I'm writing with now, in hopes that my story reaches someone, and if you're reading this, whoever you are, then I guess it has.

Whenever someone wants to shower, they kick me out of my cell and I have to wait until they're done showering before returning. If you're wondering why some of these pages are wet, that's why.

Anyway, I'm their first human sacrifice.

They'll impale me on the giant fish hook. They'll string me up and force me to swim out into the river. The red and white bobber that can float three-hundred pounds will prevent the hook from sinking me, at least until I swam far enough out for the blood bass to come for me. This is how Bob planned on increasing his supplies of black slime, which he'd been acquiring by tossing his unlucky acolytes into the river, a method that was both inefficient and dangerous. Now, with a refined method, Bob would lead his people into a new dark age. "You'll have the honor of being the first of many sacrifices," he said to me, and I cherished the words, because once again I held an honored place in the eyes of Bob.

This is the end.

They're coming to take me down to the river.

I leave this notebook in the shower that's like my final resting place.

In spite of myself and all Bob has done to me, I hope things work out for him.

Postscript from the Dead

When you die, as you're passing from the earthly life to the next, a single memory from your lifetime comes roaring back to you, like a scream from a you-shaped void. I'm technically dead now, and if you've read this far, then it means you'll soon be dead -- or undead -- too. Don't worry. There are perks to this underwater kingdom. The life of a ghost fish, or whatever we are, isn't so bad. And when our god awakens from his slumbering depths in the Pacific, the oceans and rivers of the earth will rise up and overtake the land. We will inherit the earth.

But about that last memory.

It's not always a good one.

If you've ever nearly drowned or had a close encounter with something monstrous (excluding the present), your brain will likely carry you back to one of those times. I know. You're in excruciating pain. Panicked. I was in your position not too long ago. Impaled on a giant fishing hook, drifting under an absurdly large red and white bobber. Don't worry. The last memory isn't all bad. Me, I remembered a time in South Africa, fishing a lower stretch of the Great Fish River on the Eastern Cape. I was fishing for grunter alone. I put a nice fish in the boat early on, but the fishing slowed. I had a couple beers and grew tired under the hot midday sun. I decide to lie back and nap before fishing the evening bite. Sometime later, I awoke to a strange sound. My boat had drifted into a group of hippos. I tried to gun it out of there, but I flooded the motor. The noise agitated the hippos, and one of them flipped my boat. Somehow, I swam to the far shore. I'd lost my boat, my fishing gear, the nice grunter I'd caught, but I came out with my life. There was an old man who lived in a cave on the far side of the Great Fish River, and he watched this whole scene go down. As I sat there on the sand, sputtering and in shock, shivering, he approached me and gestured for me to follow him. For reasons I still don't understand, I walked back with him to his cave, where he cooked us a grunter twice the size of the one I'd caught over coals. We ate the fish in silence and then got drunk on some type of sour fermented beer that he'd made himself. We drank until we couldn't stand up, and then we passed out by the dying fire. I awoke the next morning with the worst hangover of my life, but that night in the cave with the old man was worth it. As I died, I relived that day on the river, that night in the cave. I hope you find a memory like that of your own. You'll want to go there when I sink my teeth in. Right...about...now.

Bobber down.

Acknowledgments

Special thanks to the Mellon Foundation, Gary Lucas, Gabino Iglesias, Shane McKenzie, Paul Wessels, Robert Berold, Stacy Hardy, Morgan Trauernicht, Longleat, and most of all, Kirsten Alene Pierce and Peablossom.

About the Author

Cameron Pierce is the Wonderland Book Award-winning author of thirteen books, including *Our Love Will Go the Way of the Salmon* and *Bottom Feeders* (w/ Adam Cesare). His work has appeared in *Gray's Sporting Journal*, *Letters to Lovecraft*, *Dark Discoveries*, *Giallo Fantastique*, and many other publications. He is also the editor of the groundbreaking anthology *The Best Bizarro Fiction of the Decade*. Pierce lives in Astoria, Oregon with his wife and daughter.